THE JANITOR

By   Russell Kinchen

ABOUT THE AUTHOR

Russell Kinchen was born in Chicago, Illinois, the youngest of twelve, most introverted of the bunch, He was reading newspapers before the age of five. When his siblings were too busy to teach him about the ways of the world, he taught himself a series of things including how to play different musical instruments, and how to draw. Throughout his life, he had various jobs from a bathroom attendant at a gym to a library page. Russell wrote lyrics and poems on notepads or anything that had space for him to write on to express his Imagination. Russell moved to Minnesota in 2001 worked as a janitor and became a State worker. In 2010 he decided to write a fictional story about a janitor. The novel is loosely based on his experience working for a janitorial service in Saint Paul Minnesota.

Acknowledgment

I would like to give thanks to Shirley Kinchen for the gift of life, to my brother Raymond for always giving me advice, to my cats Max, Molly, and Myla for putting up with my moody self! To Charisma and Sammie for being there when I needed to vent, to JB who Dared me into creating something different. And to The Creator because without him, or her, anything and everything would not be possible.

Chapter 1: Take What You Can

"Mr. Nathan Smith," shouted the caseworker.

Nate got up after a half-an-hour wait on a hard plastic chair, the back of his shirt wrinkled and his ass felt numb. He gravitated toward the worker, as if they "the caseworkers," were the shepherds of the weary and broke.

"Come this way, please have a seat," said the worker.

"OK," said Nate.

"How are you?" asked the worker.

"Fine, thank you for asking replied Nate. "No air today, huh?"

"No, it's on the blink, and it should be repaired tomorrow said the worker.

"May I have a piece of

candy?" asked Nate.

"Sure, take as much as you like," responded the worker.

As Nate partook in the assortment of candy, he noticed her family portrait And Said, "Nice picture."

She said "Thanks. Let me get your file."

As Nate gazed around, he noticed a layer of dust on top of the cubicles that should have been cleaned by the janitorial staff. In his head, he examined his OCD and said to himself, "I hate sloppy work. I could do their job better for half the pay." *Sometimes be careful of what you wish for.*

"OK, I got your file." The caseworker glanced to see Nate's status and asked, "How's your mother doing?"

"The same, no improvements. Sometimes it breaks my heart that my mom doesn't even know who I am." Nate sighed and teared up, remembering the good times, from Holidays to birthdays.

"Sorry to hear that. But I have good news for you."

Nate perked up in his chair, and said: "You do?"

"I have a part-time position available. It's minimum wage. For a cleaning company. They have five accounts in the twin-cities."

With no questions asked, Nate said, "I'll take it."

She said, "Fine, I'll fax over your records. I just have some paperwork for you to sign, then I can send you on your way."

"Thank you," said Nate with the biggest smile on his face as he signed the papers.

"Ok Nate, that's it. Here's the number and address so go in tomorrow after 4, and you have a good rest of your day."

"You as well, and thanks again," said Nate. He rose from his seat a new, happy refreshed, man.

On his way to exit, he bumped into a small, 5-foot 6-inch, scrawny guy. Nate quickly said "I'm so sorry sir. I didn't see you."

The guy looked up at Nate and said, *"Don't I know you? Did you go to Central High School?"*

"Yeah. Aren't you Paul?" Nate replied.

"Yeah, aren't you Nathan? Yep, oh man. Do you remember Stacy?

"Yeah, you guys were an item," said Nate.

Paul sulked and said, *"I married her."*

"Congrats," said Nate.

Paul said, *"Thanks,"* with a sarcastic look on his face like a judge had given him a life sentence.

"Oh, well, I best to get going so I can tell my mom the good news.

"What happened?" Asked Paul.

"I got a job. It's part-time, but it's something! Nate said.

"Congratulation" I have a 1:45 appointment Paul said.

"Good luck," said Nate.

"Thanks," said Paul.

"See you around," said Nate.

"Yep," Said Paul.

Paul walked up and said to the receptionist, *"I have a 1:45 appointment."*

"What's your name?" inquired the receptionist.

"Paul Nelson,"

"OK, you can have a seat. I'll let your worker know you're here."

"Thanks," said Paul.

When he first came through the door, Paul had seen the chair where he wanted to sit.
A very observant person, perhaps even hyper-vigilant, Paul was always looking out of the corner of his eyes, scanning everything and anything. He would also examine the bus for seats available before it was in front of him. This is something he always has done since he was a kid. Back then it was essential for him to be sharp, to know when and where his abuse was coming from.

Chapter 2: Tortured Soul

Paul came from a family of five, three brothers and two sisters. He was the middle child, which meant special treatment eluded him. Paul was invisible. When Christmas came, all the other children would get everything they asked for - the best and the newest toys. As for Paul, he would get a broom, vacuum or a cheap dollar store trinket. His holiday requests always fell on deaf ears.

For the others, their childhoods were like a vacation on

Easy Street. As for Paul, all chores were given out to him. Whenever he protested, out came the wolves, even some of the siblings pitted against him. They would make up stories about things he said or broke, just to piss off his parents so the punishments wouldn't let up.

Whenever the family would go to a restaurant, they would all order burgers, fries, and shakes. For Paul, they would cancel his order. For the time being Paul felt like a foster child. Once everyone began eating Paul would sit there with the most lost look on his face as his tummy rumbled from hunger.

Sometimes other patrons would notice the neglect and try to buy him something to eat. "Hey, little buddy how about a kid's meal? What kind of drink would you like?"

Paul would then smile than frown as his parents would tell the well-intentioned patrons loudly to **"Mind your fucking business."**

Then Later, Paul went back to "his personal Hell." Outsiders looking in would call him "a boy Cinderella." They would have him dust, clean and wipe the house from top to bottom.

One of the other things they would do to Paul was thrown clean dishes in the dirty dishes sink just to keep him busy. Bathroom duties were the worst. The parents would egg the kids to purposely miss the toilet, so Paul had to clean up puddles of urine and piles of excrement off the floor and toilet seat and smears of shit on the walls. To be really mean they would spell Paul's name out in feces. In the midst of all this anarchy, Paul did have one Person on his side, his youngest sister, Angie.

Angie was born with a heart

defect. She always helped Paul, with food when he's hungry, a half sandwich here, a piece of bacon there, and she would sneak a bottle of water for him when no one was looking. Even with his chores with no questions asked. Paul loves his sister dearly. She was the angel he needed in his life of strife. Paul's father, Charlie, worked in a Toy factory, building things to bring kids happiness. What irony, once a year the Toy Company host a family picnic for all the employees. Paul enjoyed the picnics because it gave him a chance to get away from the madness of his home. To everyone's surprise, Paul got to go to the picnics due to Charlie's fear of his boss. So, all the kids were lectured before they went: behave; don't act a fool, and be seen not heard: "blah, blah, blah." There were a great variety of foods, snacks, and games at the function. Paul was in heaven. This was his Christmas and birthday all rolled up in one. For once a year Paul felt like a kid instead of a slave.

Also, at the picnic, Paul got a chance to hang with his sister. *"Hey Angie, how are you on this beautiful day?*

"I'm good," Angie replied.
"How are you, Paul? *I'm better
now.* Whoa, that Barbeque smells
and looks so good! Oh, they made
Jell-O. I love Jell-O. Sorry for
running off at the mouth about the
food. It's just that mom and dad
don't make stuff like this at home
said, Angie.

"I wouldn't know," replied
Paul.

"I know......... sorry," But I
look out for you because I love you
said, Angie

"And I love you too Angie,"
Paul replied, as he hugged his sister

as his oldest brother frowned.
"Come with, let's sit down and talk
some more, um, over here, "said
Angie as she grabbed Paul's hand
and dragged him to the closest
bench.

"How's school?" asked Paul.

"It's good. We're doing Arts
and crafts and working on our
letters and numbers," said Angie.

*"Oh cool" "What grade are
you in?"* said Paul.

"First grade," Angie answered.

*"Wow, we live in the same
house, and we don't know much*

about each other, said Paul as he looked at the sky and sighed while rubbing his head in confusion.

"Oh, it's ok. We have forever to find out more," said Angie. "What grade are you in Paul?"

"7th" you want to know what the funniest thing is, Angie? I like school more than home, " Paul said.

"Yeah" replied Angie. "Don't know why mom, dad, and our brothers and sisters are so mean to you?" Angie questioned.

Hmm don't know, " replied Paul.

"Hey everybody, we're about to start the dodgeball games. Everyone who's ten and older line up here said the announcer over the loudspeaker. Paul rose from the bench like a gladiator. One of the games Paul liked to play was dodgeball.

It's the one game where he could release his stress, and lord knows he needs it.

When Paul had the ball in his hands, no one wanted to be in his way. He threw the ball with the might of a grown man. Paul didn't strike the kids he didn't know, just siblings who tormented him daily.

There goes the youngest brother in his scope whoop----Wham, he went down with the quickness of light. Then the oldest sister, Wham, she got checked on the chin. You would have thought her head would have come off with the speed of the ball.

Then the oldest brother was in his scope. Whoop, he missed. Whoop, swoop, again. His brother was too quick for Paul, but Paul was determined to hit his mark. He figured he could take his anger out in this game without getting into trouble. After an hour, everyone had a turn and grew exhausted, but Paul wasn't tired at all. He had one goal, to take his big brother down no matter what! But his big brother had the ball next, and his big brother had the opposite goal, to take Paul down. His big brother hated Paul because Paul was the family doormat and his brother had the responsibility and great pleasure of treating Paul like shit. But Paul was on point, dodging his brother's attack. Paul would be damned if he would be the one to go down.

Something happens in a flash.
Paul was locked in his brother's sight.
He looked at Paul. Paul looked

back. Like a great western shoot-out, someone had to go down.

Paul darted out of the way as his brother released the ball at hyper-speed. At this moment, Angie, Paul's angel, came out from nowhere. Angie naturally worried that her brother was hungry and had returned with a plate of food of chicken spaghetti, and Jell-O. Angie was carefully handing the plate for Paul and didn't see the ball coming toward her. The ball hit her in the head, so hard that her little neck snapped back. She collapsed as the air, and life left her little body.

The park fell silent.

Chapter 3:

The Opportunity

"Have a seat, Paul," said the caseworker. "How are you?"

Paul grumbled, *"Ok I guess. Didn't grab breakfast, so I'm a little peckish, sorry if I seem out of it."*

"No problem. Everyone seems to be out of it because of this unbearable weather.

"Oh, that's what that is, I thought it was me," replied Paul.

"Nah, it's the central air, unless you're the first male to go through menopause. Oh, I'm sorry, that was inappropriate," interjected the worker.

"No problem, There nothing wrong with a little humor."

"Well, I have good news for you to smile about," the caseworker said.

"Hmm," said Paul, without any facial expression.

"Ok, let's take a look at your file Paul," said the worker as she opened his folder.

Paul's heart beating like it wanted to escape out of his chest, and her words slowed like a car in rush hour traffic "PAAAAAUUUUULLLLLLL IIIIIIIIT SEEEEEEEEEEEMS TTHHHHHHHHHAAAAAAT

IIIIIIIIIIIIIIIIIIIIIIIIIIIIIIIIIIIIIIIIIIIIIIII
HHHHHHAAAAAAAAAAAAAAA
VVVVVE found something for
you."

Paul was so nervous that the
sound of his pulse blocked his ears
from hearing the good news, so
Paul asked: *"could you repeat that,*
please?"

"I said I found something for
you,"

"It's a small part-time
position." the worker replied,

"Oh," said Paul.

"It's a cleaning job you don't
have any problems with that do
you?"

"Nope. I do all the chores at

home. I've been cleaning my whole

life. I grew up with messy people,

real pigs, said Paul

Sorry to hear that," responded

the worker, "but it sounds you have

developed some valuable skills."

"Yes indeed," "I'm willing

and able, and for things I don't

know how to do, I'm a fast learner

responded Paul.

"Well it's for $7.25 an hour,

and part-time." The worker

informed Paul.

"Something's better than

nothing

Now my wife can somewhat

get off my astronaut   I

mean case, sorry," said Paul.

"No problem, all I have to do is fax over your info, just go in tomorrow to fill out the application and good luck!

"Thanks," said Paul.

He left the Workforce Center with a smile on his face.

"I hope Stacey will be proud of me. She should be, maybe I'll get some loving tonight," Paul thought. As he headed down his block, then noticed a parcel truck in his driveway. "I hope he's delivering something good."

Inside the house, Stacey was fucking the parcel man. She moans, "Fuck me. Ooh, fuck me harder. Damn, you have such a big cock.

My husband is such a loser with a tiny prick that can't even stay hard for two minutes but thank God for you giving me such a big package for my starving pussy. Fuck me hard!! Oh, yeah."

Outside, Paul tries his keys, but no luck. The keys turned, but the door won't open as if something was propped in front the door. Paul worked his keys for 2 minutes straight. Then he knocks and heard a shift by the door. Then emerges the parcel man with sweat on his upper lip and forehead. Paul stutters, *"Hello did you bring us something good?"*

With a grin on his face, the

parcel man responded, "Oh, yeah. I delivered a package to your wife," then he got in his truck.

Paul waved with a smile on his face and said, *"Thanks."* The parcel guy had a puzzled look on his face as he pulled off.

Paul kept that smile still on his face, entered his home and saw his wife panting and gasping and fixing her hair with her nightgown on. "What are you looking at dumb-ass? What did you do today? Did you get a job? She said, Paul frantically said, *"Yes, babe!!!*

"Bout time," Stacey said. *I thought we can make love tonight* to celebrate," said Paul.

Stacey laughed, "Ha, you wish.

"Please" begged Paul, not tonight
my pussy hurts from a lot of
chafing, maybe from a tampon or
something." Then Stacey walked off
with a smile on her face.

I don't know why I got married but
what choice did I have? The lessor
of the two evils. All the work around
here is done by me.   I mow the
lawn, shovel the snow, recycle, and
pick up any trash on the sidewalks
all year around. I have invested my
time into beautifying this block, and
not one thanks me, Mumbled Paul,'

"Who the fuck are you talking
to?" asked Stacey, with her cell

phone in hand click-clacking away.

"Oh, nothing," said Paul. *"Damn why doesn't she divorce me and marry her damn phone? It will get more action than me since I don't vibrate said Paul with a* crooked smile then shook his head in disbelief of the human disconnect do to gadgets.

CHAPTER 4: MARRIED LIFE

It started in high school. Paul was shy, with one friend -Nate. Sometimes you don't get to pick your girlfriend. She'll pick you especially if you're Weak. It starts with carrying her books, Do my homework! Paint my nails! Do my chores and Kiss my ass.

She had him wrapped around her finger like a band-aid.

He would do anything for her, even fight anyone she didn't like. One day she told him to kick this one guy's ass that picked on her in class. Not knowing his teasing was a form of admiration but he could've shot straight from the hip now he has a busted lip.

Through life he had been rejected and neglected, anyone would have killed to be in his shoes now. And why not, he had a hot 5-foot 2 sexy blonde that looked like Kelly Bundy. She hooked him like a worm, and all it took was a little sex. Now she has a lifelong sucker. Straight out of high school they got a cheap storefront apartment. Paul found odd jobs to pay the bills as Stacey attended community college. Paul was just so happy to get out of that hell whole he grew up in.

Now goes the term, 'the lesser of two evils.' It didn't start off all bad. They were like Bonnie and Clyde. They did what they had to do to keep everything afloat. From Delinquent bank loans, bouncing checks and shoplifting. They were closer than ever, and no matter what Paul didn't want to mess it up with disagreements or arguments, so he knew the boundaries.

When Stacey and Paul got married, his family didn't have any disagreement because they saw how she controlled him and it made them smile in the way of the Olympians passing the torch of power. Her family didn't care because they were going to the Justice of the Peace,150.00 bucks and a blood test. What more could you ask for?

On June 13th, Paul and Stacey were married, on a

very stormy and windy day. If that wasn't a sign, I don't know what could have been, that this union wasn't meant to be. They couldn't afford a real honeymoon, so they went bowling and got a room at a cheesy motel.

They had a blast. Paul let Stacey win every game because she was the boss, and it didn't hurt she was a damn good bowler. Inside his head, he said, "*Man, I finally did it. I found a jewel.*" He never smiled like as a child.

He must have cracked his
face from the new
expression using muscles
he hadn't before.
It was indeed a magical
night, at least for the
moment. They arrived at
the motel to check in for
the night. Paul noticed the
vending machines and
asked his new bride *did she*
want anything after they
got settled?

She said, "Yes, but let
me get the snacks."

He said *"Ok. I'm*
going to jump in the

shower. Could you get some chips, pop, and peanut butter cups? Let me get some change for you."

She said, "No, I got it. Just get in the shower, Mr.!!"

He laughed and said, *"Ok my love."*

As he cut the water on, she rushed out the door like the place was on fire, but she wasn't going to the machines. She was heading to the lobby for something else. Earlier, as Stacey and Paul were checking in, she was checking out the motel clerk.   She had winked at him, and quickly slipped him a note, that stated: "I'll be back in 30 minutes." Then the guy smiled.

But little did she know he called a couple of his best buds. So the clerk told them to chill in the office behind the front desk. Stacey got off the elevator. Full of lust, she walked to the front desk looking for the clerk and there he was sitting at the counter.

He said, "Hi, let me put up a 'Be Right Back sign.

She said, "Ok, but hurry. My husband is in the shower." He said, "Ok.", I got a surprise for you.

She said, "What is it?"

He said, "A wedding gift."

"Oh, really?" she said.

He said, "Yeah." So he cut the lights on. There

were his two friends, in the buff.

She said, "Fuck yeah, I love gifts."

As the sex romp starts, Paul is starting his shower thinking of the sex he's about to have. As he takes the bar of soap out of the wrapper, the guy's downstairs is taking the clothes off Stacey.   As Paul gets his face towel wet to soap up, the guys get their cocks drenched from Stacey sucking them off two at a time. As Paul start

soaping up his body frame,
the guys are stretching
Stacey walls out of shape
from double penetration.
As Paul dries off after his
shower, Stacey wipes off
the cum-shower the guys
gave her. Paul opened the
bathroom door and said
hmm she's not back yet?
Minutes later Stacey gets
on the elevator to head back
to the room. Paul gets
under the cover nodding his
head thinking *"Oh yeah."*
Stacey comes back to the
suite, then walks straight

into the Bathroom.

"Where are the snacks, why are you panting, and what took you so long?" Said, Paul

What's up with the thousand questions?? if you must know "Someone was chasing me, so I ran and hid, that's why," explained Stacey.

"Oh, my word! Are you ok? Said, Paul."

"Oh yes, yes, I am," said Stacey with a smirk. "I need to take a shower sweetie."

"Ok." Paul laid there in bed with great anticipation of making love for the first time as newlyweds.

Stacey got out of the shower in 7 minutes, got dressed and slid into bed and slid next to Paul, and turned her head to him and said "Not tonight. I got a migraine."

Paul turned away to his side, *Ok, maybe tomorrow,* I hope your head gets better." then he teared up.

A month later they won the lottery for $150,000 and purchased a Foreclosed home for $82,000. Stacey took control of the remaining funds! And bought herself: Furs, diamonds, expensive shoes and purses without checking the accounts. Sadly, Paul couldn't buy any new clothes, but underwear and socks. And one day she sat on his reading glasses, and wouldn't buy him a new pair or give him the repair cost, so he begged the outlet to replace the frames stem. Luckily, they were covered for a one-year frame repair.   Being thankful for little mercies, then he found out she sank all the accounts into the negative.

CHAPTER 5:

The start of something new

Paul didn't sleep well last night due to new job jitters. It's quite common to ponder what is in store for you: new environment, rules, structure and performing up to par promptly. That's enough pressure that could make a fish shit a brick.

Paul showed up an hour early to check everything out and get on the right side of the bosses. He walked to the front desk and said, *"Hello, my name is Paul, I'm here to see Jolene."*

The receptionist looked

puzzled. Then she said, "Oh, for the cleaning crew.

I'll call them to let them know you're here."

Paul said, *"Thanks."* Then he sat down. Five minutes passed, and Paul was getting anxious. His leg was jumping like a jack-hammer breaking up cement, as he pondered his new employment.

Then, suddenly, this short, balding man with a t-shirt and high-water jeans appeared. He went to the receptionist and asked. "Is that him?"

She said, "Yep."

Then he walked over to Paul and held out his hand and said, "Hi, my name is Larry and yours?"

"Pa, Pa, Paul." When he gets nervous, he has a slight stutter.

As they shook hands, "Nice to meet you, Paul. I'm the owner of the cleaning company C.C.M. Come this way. Paul followed as he examined his new surroundings, as they walked down and through a series of hallways and doors that led them to a small office. "Have a seat," said Larry. Paul sat down and was all ears. I'm going to ask you a couple of questions, then you will start your training."

"Yes sir," Paul nervously said.

"Do you have any cleaning experience?"

"No, just at home. I do all the housework Duties.   My wife isn't any good at that kind of stuff, and I can't stand a dirty home. I've been cleaning since I was a child. I guess you can say I was born to clean or cry trying to keep it clean."

Larry laughed, Then Paul laughed. well, I think you'll fit well in here." Then he said, "I got a couple more things to run by you. the things that will get you in trouble and fired: No stealing, no touching items on the desks, except for when your dusting. no touching the computers, or being constantly late, caught leaving early and using cell phones that's also a call for termination."

"Well, you wouldn't have to worry about me. I don't steal, and I hate computers, but my wife loves them. She's always on those social media sites. God knows who she's chatting with. I feel that she'll

choose that over her husband and that's a shame, but anyway sorry to bore you with my life," said Paul. "Okay," said Larry. "You got the jest of it. You work from 4:30 PM to 8:30 PM Monday through Friday and you get a fifteen-minute break at 7:00 to 7:15.

"Sounds excellent. said, Paul.

"Let me take you to your assigned building, said Larry.

"OK, replied Paul

They walked across the parking lot. Larry pulled out his access badge to scan the door, then they entered the basement of the office building, Larry had a cold chill in his spine, then told Paul.

I've heard old timers say "When you get a chill down your back, someone's walking on your grave Paul said.

"Huh," said Larry. Well, I'm not superstitious, and besides, I'm getting cremated." They both laughed as they traveled upstairs to the cafeteria. Paul's eyes widened as he glanced nervously at his new co-workers. Larry told Paul to have a seat and wait until 4:30, "Then Jolene will get you started."

"Yes, sir." Then he sat down, feeling out of place like a kindergartner on his first day of school. Paul's an avid

clock-watcher, counting the minutes and seconds and, if he could, the milliseconds, till he meets his supervisor and start work.

It was 4:15 and Paul just glanced over the heads of some of his co-workers, just to absorb the atmosphere. Then entered a 5 foot 2, frizzed hair brunette with a voice that would annoy a monk and peel paint off a wall. "You must be Paul. *Yes, I am*, I am Jolene, your new boss. A lot of people say I'm a cool boss. I'm really one with the staff. We're all janitors!! Isn't that right, Ricky?" asked Jolene.

"Yep, she's a cool boss. She hardly yells at me," agreed Ricky with a grin.

"Ok, we processed your application, and now all we need is a photocopy of your I.D," said Jolene.

Paul pulled out his wallet and grabbed his driver's license, then passed it to Jolene and in the process, knocked over a co-workers soda. *"Ah man!"* said Paul frantically. *"I'm so sorry,"* as he quickly dabbed up the soda on the table. *"I'll buy you another one."*

"*Oh, man not on my first day. I'm fucking up*," ran through his head as he teared up cleaning the mess.'

The guy said to Paul, "It's no problem." But Paul didn't hear him. All Paul heard was his wife telling him he's worthless and a mistake, which his mom should have taken care of with a wire coat hanger!!

4:30 popped up and everyone scattered to their assigned Floors but Paul, Jolene, and George. "Sign in here Paul, then George will train you in today, here's your license. And by the way, you're cleaning bathrooms!!!"

Paul silently sulked and dragging his feet to the area….George was one of the best trainers and well liked.   George told Paul, "It's an easy job once you

get the hang of it. Follow me.
There's going to be two carts that
you'll use Daily.   One for toiletries
and one for the mop and broom."

"*Ok,*" said Paul.

You have 7 sets of bathrooms
to clean, so it shouldn't take you
more than 25 minutes per floor to
clean.

Paul and George started on the 6th
floor.
The first thing to do is grab the dust
broom."

Paul nervously detached the broom
from the cart bracket.

"Ok, now I need you to sweep
out all of the bathrooms before we
start the training, so each person

who cleans a floor can vacuum up the paper, debris from the bathroom instructed George. Paul left, and George frantically called Paul as he walked into the women's bathroom. "You have to knock and knock hard and listen good before entering a women's bathroom," "Sorry, I should have told you," explained George.

"No problem, George. I should have known better myself," Paul said before he knocked on the women's door. Luckily it was empty when he swept it out. As Paul went into the men's room, George crept to the ladies to see how Paul did, it was spotless. Then George waited

for Paul to finish the first task. Usually, it takes 15 minutes to sweep out all of them, plus the wait time for the ladies room. So George figured he had time to get on his phone and talk to his sweetheart Rosa.

"Hello, this is George. Is Rosa home?"

"Hold on," said her mom.

"Hi, George. Hey sweetie, how are you?" asked Rosa.

"Good, I'm good, just training a new guy," replied George.

"How is he doing?" asked Rosa.

"Good so far, just a little strange," replied George.

"What time you get off of work tonight?" asked Rosa.

"I don't know," said George. Usually, 8:30 but Larry was talking about a shampoo job at another building,

"Ah, I miss you so much," said Rosa.

"I miss you too, but I will let you know Hun.

"Done," interjected Paul.

"Oh, you scared me."

"Talk to you later my love, said, George.

"Wow, that was quick.

"Thanks. I finished all 14 bathrooms in less than 7 minutes," said Paul.

"Well that's a record for speed!" replied George.

"Thanks," said Paul.

"Well, let's stop back patting and start cleaning these bathrooms," directed George.

"Ok," Paul responded.

"Well, the first thing is to check the stock of toilet paper and hand towels, then clean the sinks and then the toilets and mop," George instructed.

Chapter 6:

Leaps and Discouragement

I weep silently of the past and loudly of my future in the midst of wolves. They can smell fear and blood.

Paul came home after his crowning achievement, doing excellent on his first day at his new job. Again, he's locked out, so he tries, and tries again. This time, the Electric Company is making a late night repair, and Paul starts to wonder. Not that he's slow, just that he's a fool for love. But when it's turning sour, he gets smarter each hour.

"SO, WHAT'S WRONG WITH THE ELECTRICITY!!!" said Paul in a vigorous tone.

"We had an outage," said Stacey.

"Hmmm, sure," said Paul with his lips twisted. *"So, what did he do, screw in his bulb in a rotten socket?* said Paul, just for once, made a funny.

"So how was your first day, Hun?" asked Stacey.

Paul grumbled," It *was ok."*

"Aren't you going to ask me about my day?" said Stacey.

"Nope, not really," said Paul.

"I know how your day went whenever I just see a serviceman leave here. I JUST FUCKING KNOW."

As he stormed off to the den. Stacey stood speechless.   Paul always recluses himself when he's down, but this time it was different because he felt like he was in control for once.

He sat in his favorite chair, it was comforting to him, like a blanket from his childhood. It was a beaten down old and tethered, but it was his, mainly 'because it was like him. He looked up and noticed a manila envelope in between the stack of boxes in the closet. So, he got up and opened the content and saw the certificates of his academic achievements and a series of discarded photos.

Paul took his time

organizing them into three stacks by Likes, dislikes and hated. He first went through the drawings: a series of angry scribblings, curse words, knives, blood, body parts, and a little boy smiling. In the midst of static and pain, was a drawing of a girl angel, hovering over the morbid landscapes. In another pile lay his stack of certificates. Throughout his upbringing in an uneven abusive home, Paul excelled in school - the only place he felt safe and liked, with straight A's

and numerous accolades.

One award was for poetry,

for his short poem called,

"What Love Means to Me."

Love means a lot to some,

But not much to the

lonely, the rejected

and the abused.

Choose not to believe

in such fables,

Like a fat guy barely

sliding down a

chimney

Giving away free

gifts,

For your ability to

turn the other cheek

And not bash people

skulls in

For being jerks to you

all year long,

Wow, a toy truck for

all that teeth grinding.

Thanks! The dentist

will be pleased.

I dream that love

should be people caring,

being genuine,   and Doing

good things because they

want to

Not because they

must.

In my nightmares that

scare, I awake after I shake

To realize that was a

lovely dream.

A big sigh fell out of

Paul's mouth as he pressed

on, digging through the

folder of his childhood.

Then, he went through a

bunch of photos that were

bound by a bit of string.

Paul was cut out of almost

everyone that he had

flipped through. You saw Paul's arm, top of his head and a leg, except for one picture, where he and his sister were a duo, hugging for the camera. That, of course, was his favorite. Even though he was snaggle-toothed, he still smiled for the picture.

As Paul plucked his favorite from the bunch, the rest were set aside for disposal. He slid the manila folder back into the closet, stretched his legs, then grabbed the bunch of unwanted photos and his favorite and left the room. Paul noticed, out of the corner of his eye, his wife was closing her laptop quick to hide her secrets, like they were really secrets. Then Stacey asked Paul where was he going and what was he doing. He said nothing, as he left home with a smirk on his face.

Once outside, he ventured to the backyard. *There goes my arm, which I should have strangled those fuckers with, and my leg, I should have kicked them to death with steeled toed boots, whoosh.* "He felt great setting his family photos on fire

Paul ventured up the street to the local drug store. *As he walked into the store, he noticed a big bin of flowers in the front of the registers and said to himself, "not for that wife of mine. Well, maybe for her grave."* Then again, let the maggots be her garnish out loud, he said." A couple of customers overheard him and giggled with a puzzled look on they're faces.

Paul smiled at their response and then walked off to get a basket, but drew a blank as to what he needed. Then he remembered, one of the things was a picture frame. *"Hmm, what aisle could they be in?* When he found them, he pondered *too many to choose from.*

Glass ones, wooden ones, and aluminum ones. *Hmm, only the best for the best sister!"* Then he collected a couple of other items and headed home.

Paul came home with the same situation going on, Stacey with her face in her notebook on "The Book," the instrument for broken homes and hearts. But this time she didn't shut it closed. She just typed away, with her grin and attitude like she was plotting an orgy on a thong string budget.

Paul didn't pay her no mind, as he emptied out his bag on the dining room table. One item he had snuck in his pocket without being seen and PB and J and his picture frame. So, he pulled the picture out of his pocket and sat down at the table and gazed at the gorgeous woman in the structure. Paul wished that his wife was thinking, *"I bet she has a better attitude and can cook too."*

"Hmmm, what have

I done to deserve this, dear God?" he said out loud. He slides the model picture out, folded it up and slid it in his pocket, then grabbed his favorite photo and placed it carefully between the glass and the cardboard and pushed the back onto the frame.

"Stacey said, "Huh?" as she lifted her hypnotized head from the social spell of her notebook.

Paul said *nothing*, not that anyone was listening anyway He turned it over and said, *"Yes, perfect."*

"Huh?" repeated Stacey.

And Paul said, *"You're far from that, Bitch!"*

"What!!!" she said.

Paul replied, *"I said my back has an itch."*

Stacey said, "Then scratch it."

He replied, *"Yep I will with the corner of the wall, not that I would ask you for anything."*

She replied, "Good!"

"Maybe I should

apply for a postal or utility job, then we could fuck more. Hmmm?"

"I'm going to pretend I didn't hear that," Stacey said.

Paul replied, *"I'm going to pretend that wasn't true."*

"Whatever," Stacey said. "By the way, Love of my life, my friend from college is coming to visit from Chicago next week."

"Male or female?" Paul murmured.

"Male. We're just friends," Stacey said. *"You just being friends with a male is unlikely,"* Paul stated and added, *"Did you fuck him?"* ".......yes, we did, many times Laughed Stacey Just kidding, don't get your panties in a bunch." *"Well, get him a room at a hotel!!!!* Stated Paul. "Huh? It's my house too," argued Stacey. *"I'm not worried*

about the house. It's
you he wants to do!!!
Said, Paul.
"Well regardless, I
run this show, and
he's staying here, and
I dare you to
intervene said
Stacey!!!! Now, let's
straighten up around
here," demanded
Stacey.
"Well, it's not my
company, and I'll be
damned if I lift a
finger for your visitor.
And that stuff about

you running the show
is all in your head
and coming out of
your mouth."
"Please," said Stacey
with a pouting bottom
lip.
Harsh Paul just
melted like cheese in
between two slices of
bread in a skillet.
"Oh, ok only if you
give me some loving
Tonight," said Paul
"Oh, ok sure that will
definitely happen,"
replied Stacey.

Chapter 7:

As the Anger Grows.

I didn't get much sleep, which I needed for my regular shift and the overtime to help strip and wax the large mailroom floor. The floor alone is an 8-hour job. I'm running late. My wife's friend is flying in tonight, and my picture is missing. I'm slowly losing it, but I have to keep it together for hell's sake 'cause heaven turned its back on me since I was 3.

Taking a quick shower should make me feel a little better. Have to shave first. As I look in the mirror, I judge I'm a pretty handsome guy.

Why do I put up with a lot of the shit that I do? Must be mental. Got to be a psychological situation. Why do I lack confidence and allow such degradation from those foes who shove instead of love? DAMN! I nicked myself. It's bleeding badly. Hopefully, direct pressure will help. Have to shower.

As Paul slide back the shower curtain and frantically jumped in, "FUCK!!" Paul slipped and fell in the shower. *That stupid bitch left a bar of soap in the tub.* "Fuck, fuck, fuck!!!" *Damn, I'm going to be late, and I don't want to hear the voice of my boss telling me so. Shit, I don't even have time for a quick jerk. Oh well, I'll do that at work in the bathroom stall.*

Minutes later, Paul comes running out of his house like a guy caught fucking somebody's wife, no pun intended. He jumps in the car and sped off to work. Paul's soundtrack to work every day is punk music, even though he drives like he's listening to polka. *Man oh 'man, I might not make it on time. Traffic isn't so bad and the weather's good. This day still can go well. Damn this guy's on my ass like I'm a new inmate. Shit, I can't go faster.*

HONK! HONK! *Damn this dude is pissing me the fuck-off! His ass better falls back and relax.*

HONK! BOOM……. *That fucker just hit my back bumper. Damn, do I have time to kick someone's ass before work??*

George has been slaving away for the cleaning company for five long years. He's seen it all and heard it all, so he thinks, for the sake of making and earning a cheap living. He lives with his two cousins and his nephew in a modest three-bedroom house on the west side of Minneapolis.

George has always been a ladies' man, having at least three girlfriends at a time, until he met his match, Rosa. She is a strong-minded woman who won't take no shit from no one, a straight shooter when it comes to what's on her mind, in English or Spanish. That's what attracted George to her. He noticed her across the room at the club, her beauty slapped him in the face like your mother would do when you talked back to her. She was deflecting guys left and right with those tired-ass lines like, "what's your sign," etc.… But when she saw George, she melted like butter near the fire. It was a simultaneous lightning strike to their hearts. After meeting Rosa, George knew his playboy days were numbered.   She was everything he wanted, and he was everything she needed.

George was sitting at home watching Maury before work. That's one of his favorites. "You are the father," he yells with the broadest smile on his face. These are good times for George. Employed, healthy have good family and friends and a great gal in his corner. Also, he has a cat named Fred. He's a black Maine Coon, full of energy and loves any attention you give him.

While George was playing with the cat, his phone rang and rang. So he turned around on his bed and answered, "Hello."

After a slight pause, "Hi."

"Hey, mom,"

"How are you, sweetie?" Georgia asked.

"I'm good, and you?" responded George.

"I'm ok, just my arthritis is acting up."

"Oh, sorry mama. I will keep you in my prayers."

"Thanks, son."

"No problem mom, anytime, every day."

"So how's work?" Georgia asked.

"It's good, still no raise, but its work," replied George. "I guess in these days and times, I can't complain."

"I agree," said mom. "Are you getting along with your co-workers?"

"Yes, mama. Why you ask?"
"Um, this is going to sound strange dear, but I've been having some weird dreams about you.
These visions started a month ago. I picture darkness, pain, and death that surrounds your workplace. It scares me so that I cry for no reason. Sometimes When I close my eyes, I see bodies and blood everywhere.

"Oh mama," interrupted George. "I'm so sorry, but as far as work goes everything is just fine."

"Ok, but do you have any new co-workers?" asked mom.

"Um, yep, just one, Paul. He's a quiet guy, but he does the job that's needed."

"Oh, what does he look like?"

"A short guy with glasses and a small limp and married without children. What are you getting at Mom? Mom? are you ok? Are you there? Mama!!"

A slow sigh………….. "Yes, Georgie."

"Yes, I am."

"Ok, mom."

"I best to be going, son. I'm tired and weak, Georgie."

"Is everything ok Mama?

Mom?"

Click then a dial tone Hmmm
that was strange, darkness, pain and
death. sounds like a dream about a
divorce. I wonder did she take her
meds? Oh well, have to get ready
for work.

*Let's see what I should wear that's
not good because I'm stripping and
waxing floors tonight. Ok, that blue
shirt with paint on it, those dressed
down jeans with holes, and my beat
down gym shoes. Thank goodness
for A/C in the building it's supposed
to be a hot one today, oh, but they
cut it off after 5 PM, hmm. George
thought to Himself.*

Miles away Paul emerged from his car red-faced and fuming as the other guy got out his car. *"WHAT THE FUCK IS YOUR PROBLEM!!!!"* yelled Paul? (At 5 feet 5 inches, and mind you the other guy's standing at 6 feet four inches.)

"YOU'RE MY PROBLEM"!!!! You drive like a granny with severe cataracts. You better pick up your pace before I put you in your place, little shit.

Then the guy shoved Paul down to the ground as traffic whizzed around them. In shocked Paul jumped quickly to his feet

"Aaaaaaghh." Paul rushed him but he was quicker, so Paul had arms full of air.

The guy stood there and laughed with his back turned. Paul quickly jumped on his back. Then he flung Paul to the hot pavement, but luckily Paul rolled over quick because he would have been a flat pancake, as an SUV sped by with his name on it. Paul grabbed his chest to keep his heart from leaping out. Then Paul noticed, out of the corner of his eye, that the guy was headed to his trunk to grab God knows what.

So, Paul ran to his car and was fidgeting the door handle out of fear. Then Paul finally opened his door simultaneously with the closing of the guy's trunk.

As soon as Paul placed his left hand on the steering wheel and right on the key, the guy appeared at his car door like a vengeful phantom holding a gun and tapping at his window. Paul screamed, then scooted over and laid across the driver and passenger seats and kicked the door open after he grabbed the handle. The guy flew back into an 18-wheeler truck.

It happened so fast. It was like a watermelon that got smashed by

Gallagher. Paul was too scared to rise up and see what was left of the guy and if there was any proof or damage to his car. Would he be questioned and miss a day of work, or worse, jail? So he quickly got up and closed his car door and pulled off. Paul noticed a little blood on his windshield. Then he turned to his left and looked down and saw the splattered entrails of his newly found ex-foe all down the highway. He grinned as the windshield wipers started and went to work.

Paul pulled into the lot, knowing what to expect from his boss. So, he had to put his game face on if he knew what that was. As he entered the door and heard her voice.

"I DON'T KNOW WHAT TIME YOU START WORK.

BUT WE START AT 4:30. IF WE DIDN'T NEED YOU TO HELP STRIP AND WAX TONIGHT, I'll SEND YOUR ASS HOME!!!!!"

Paul said, *"Hmmm,"* and walked right past Jolene to sign in, then headed to work as her voice faded in the back of his mind and ears. Knowing he was late, he had to work fiercely fast to meet his deadline for the new job. Stripping and waxing floors is not Paul's favorite. He likes to clean, and only clean. But this post can change not knowing what's in store from one day to the next. So, stripping and waxing is not new to Paul but hates the smell, so he wears a mask.

"Hey, Paul," said George "ready to do this stinky job."

"Yeah, I guess," said Paul.

"How was your day?" George asked.

"It was good, besides being a little late. Damn traffic! It can be murderous sometimes."

"Yeah, I guess," said George. "Jolene was hot, talking about you. She said you where flipping late, and you had the nerve to have an attitude. 'Blah, blah, blah.' you know?"

"Yeah she talks too damn much, she's loud and shrill. Man, I think I'm married to her," said Paul.

George laughed then gathered the equipment. One mop bucket, two mops, two plastic bags, buffing pads, rotary, edging blade, wet vacuum and stripping block. 8 hours later the dull and listless floor was sparkling and shining.

George says, "Whew, they don't pay me enough for this hard labor.

Paul said, *"Yep, but it's work,"* as *he holds the edging blade saying this would make a good murder weapon with a smile on his face.*

George pretends he didn't hear the odd statement from Paul, as he thinks of only leaving work and making love to his sweet Rosa. And on the other hand, Paul is dreading, not knowing what to expect in his unstable domain.

"Have a good night, Paul. I'll see you tomorrow, and be on time." Then they both laughed.

"Thanks, you too."

Paul got home and looked around his house for any luggage and got happy when he didn't see any. Then, all of a sudden, he heard the friend's voice.   Paul paused, as if he was at a stop sign, then pivoted and stormed to the bedroom where they were talking. Paul stuck out his hand to greet the friend.

"Hi, I'M PAUL, Stacey's husband. I don't know if she mentions me to you. Paul damn near took the guys hand off with a crushing shake.

"Gulp," said the guy nervously.
"Yes, she talked about you. Nice to
meet you, Paul," said Ross.

"Anyway," said Paul, *"let's get you
set up in the guest room because
this is our room and this room is off
limits."*

Stacey sighed and rolled her eyes.
Paul gave her a stern look of death
as he helped Ross gather his bags
out of the bedroom.

"Ok," as Paul opened the door of
the guest room, *"this is your room
and how long are you planning to
stay here in Minnesota?"*

"Um, a week I think," said Ross.

"Hmm, well, I know about you and my wife being friends in school, but it's going to stay like that this week you get my drift!!! Said, Paul.

"Yep, I got you loud and clear," said Ross.

"Sleep tight. Holler if you need something," Paul said.

"Ok, I will," said Ross.

Paul returned to the bedroom to get in his pajamas and was ready to hear a mouthful from Stacey.

As he opened his drawer, she opened her mouth. "That was fucked up. That was really uncalled for."

"Hmm, that was really disrespectful to even invite a man to our house knowing that we're having problems.

"What? We're doing ok," responded Stacey.

"Huh?? Said, Paul. *We don't make love anymore. We don't communicate. I would have been*

better off if I married my hand. Besides, it's safer and the worst case I could get a blister, but from you, I could get an STD."

"Not fucking funny," said Stacey.

"Not trying to be, but anyway where fucking tonight."

"Ha ha ha, I'm on my period. Good luck with your hand."

"Well, your mouth's not bleeding."

"Yuck, I don't do that. Come again," responded Stacey.

"Hmm, ok." Then Paul went to the kitchen to get something quick to eat and drink.

Paul is always thinking ahead so he figured to pour his energy drink into a glass and throw away the Can because she is going to believe that he would be getting sleepy soon, so she can creep. But not tonight. He returned to the bedroom with a sandwich and drink and sat on the bed and started chewing.

"Ugh, I hate the way you chew," said Stacey in disgust.

"Fuck you! I hate the way you breathe!! Retorted Paul as he took another bite with a smile and

chewed harder.

Then Paul looked over at Stacey while smacking his lips, *"Who are you texting?* "None of your fucking business."

"Oh really? I hope it's not your friend."

"What's it to you anyway?

"I'll break your phone."

"And I'll get another one," said Stacey.

"Ok then do that then!!!"

"I'm done talking to you, Paul."

"Promise me, would you, please?" said Paul.

Chapter 8:

The Hidden Habit

Nate just started with the company.
Due to over hiring his start time was
postpone, the timing was right
because he had to put his mother in
a nursing home. Her condition had
worsened, and with him working,
he couldn't take care of her at
home.

Nate works in the building across
the lot from George and Paul, but
the good thing is he doesn't have
Jolene as a supervisor. It's nice and
quiet over there until she visits her
husband Larry, but Nate won't see

or hear her that much because he works on the third floor.

His job comprises of emptying the trash, vacuuming the floors, recycling, and dusting the partitions and chairs. He likes his new job because it gives him time to think and listen to music while he cleans.

Nate loves to love and to be loved, but he doesn't have time for a relationship. Paul finished his sandwich and drink,

then put the dishes away
then came back to the
bedroom and gave the evil
eye as she texted in bed.
Paul laid down and turned
in the opposite direction
from her and tried not to
fall asleep so he can catch
her creeping. But after
twelve hours of work, Paul
drifted off to dreamland.

Paul awoke an hour later
and turned around. He felt
the lump under the sheets
and discovered it was her
pillows oblong to make it

look that she was next to
him. Paul's face flushed
and his sadness covered
his anger. He teared up and
extended his quivering
bottom lip. But she made a
second mistake by leaving
her cell phone on the bed.

Paul jotted down all the
names and numbers from
that men that sent
messages to her - including
guess who, Ross. Paul was
sick to his stomach at the
texts she sent and the ones
she received.

The exchange with Ross.

Ross: I can't wait until I fuck that hot tight pussy. Is that dumb fucker asleep yet? LOL

Stacey: Nope but soon, and you are right he's dumb and clueless. Man, I can't wait to suck and fuck that big cock.

He's got the nerve to be in my house disrespecting me. Death is too good for the both of them!

Whispered Paul as he put

the phone down.

Two hours later, she snuck
back in bed. Paul played it
cool like a winter night
and said nothing and did
nothing. Then fell back
asleep, silently crying. He
woke before the morning
alarm struck, dazed and
confused in a trance.
Stacey was up texting
early. Then she stopped,
suddenly, and asked Paul,
"What's wrong with you?"

He said, "Nothing,"

as if she didn't exist. He
dragged on like a puppet
with loose wires. Then got
into the shower, cut the
water on and just stood
there watching each bead
of water falling from the
shower head for an hour,
nor did he hear Stacey
banging on the door along
with her so-called "friend"
Ross.

I guess when you're
catatonic you couldn't hear
the world ending. When
Paul got out of the

bathroom, he just walked past the two, like panhandlers in the subway. He got dressed and left early, without eating breakfast. Paul sat in his car for a while, as Stacey looked out the window every few minutes until he pulled off.

His first stop was to the drug store to pick up shoe covers, stockings, a pack of razors and cosmetics. Then he headed to the hardware store to pick up duct tape, rope, and super

adhesive glue. And one
more stop before work, to
the women clothing store
for a dress and wig.

The store clerk
greeted him, "Hi, I'm
Amy. May I help you find
something?

"Hmmm," Paul had to
think. *"Um, my wife is sick.
And, I need a dress for her,
she's about my size and,
um, a wig if you carry
them. She lost most of her*

hairs. ”

"I'm so sorry to hear that,"
said Amy.
"Yeah, thanks. Stacey will
die soon, and I will take her
out!!!" Um, to dinner for
the last time.

So, sad to hear sir. But I
will help you find what you
need. Let's head to the wig
section. What color and
style do you need for her?"

"Medium length blonde."

"Will this one do?"

That's fine. That will work.

"You sure?"

"Yep."

"Ok, let's go to the dress section. so, you say your wife is about your size?"

"Yep."

"You look about a size 6-8. Ok, here's the rack for that size," said Amy.

"Ok, I got it from here," said Paul.

"Ok, let me know when you're ready, and I'll ring that up for you.   Oh, let me take that wig to the counter for you."

"Ok, thanks to said Paul, then he scanned for dresses. Then was met with stares, giggles and scrunched up faces, as he placed dresses against himself to get the size right.

One patron mumbled, "He

should try it on in the dressing room," then laughed. But when the commenters made their way to the counter, Amy explained then they felt terrible.

After a half an hour, Paul picked out four dresses and made his way to the counter. *"I'm done, Amy."*

"Ok, these four and the wig?"

"Yep."

Amy said, "$101.76, sir."

"Wow, ok I'll use my card, on second thought, I better use cash. Where's the closest ATM

"In the store entryway."

"Ok, I'll be right back."

"Ok."

Two minutes later Paul came back with $120.00.

Amy said, "Here's your change, $18.24. *Ok, thanks to* said, Paul. Want to be on our mailing list?"

"No, that's ok. I don't wear women's clothing." They both laughed then Amy apologized.

Paul said, *"That's all right. Ok, let me get going,"* Paul said.

"I guess I'll see you around. Let me give you my number. If you need to talk to someone for support, give me a buzz," said Amy.

"Thanks," said Paul with a big smile on his face.

"Oh, what's your name?" asked Amy.

"Um, Phil," Paul replied.

"Oh, ok, nice to meet you, Phil."

"Nice to meet you too, Amy. And thank you for your help today. You made my day

"Awe, thanks, Phil. Glad I could help. *"Ok. Bye."*

Paul walked out to his car, then opened the trunk and placed the bags inside and thought to himself. *Damn bought a lot of stuff today. I guess it's about reaching your goals even if the goal is revenge.*

No conflicts today, so no bitching from Jolene, so he thought. Soon as Paul came in, he was the butt of a joke, "Look who's on time," spouted Jolene and the workers giggled and laughed.

Paul sighed and rolled his eyes as he signed the log sheet. Then had to go to the restroom but, he thought to himself, *better take a pen and paper and sit in a stall since he has 15 minutes before the starts time. He needs to put his plans together for the "guys." the first thing he came up with was, a no-brainer, night targets, go after each victim after work.*

Since her "friend" is here for six more days, he'll keep her busy while I'll take out the other four. I'll save the best for last. The voice in his head said "*Tonight.*" Paul's stomach dropped, and his nerves kicked in. Paul got up and started his shift.

Paul was so nervous, He was sweating and panting through his shift. But his

voices kept him calm, "*You will be just fine*"
"*After the first one, the rest will be a breeze.*"

As the night grew near he got more and more nervous about the task that laid ahead for him. Paul tried talking himself out of it but thoughts of Ross fucking his wife and in his home, in his bed, the doubts turned dark. So he kept that frame of mind till the job's done.

Paul worked past his lunch break, so George had to check on him to make sure he was ok. "Hey, no break tonight?"

"Paul said, *no. I have lots to do*".

"Is everything Cool?" asked George, noticing Paul was extra nervous and dripping with sweat?

"I'm ok. It gets warm in these bathrooms sometimes. Thanks for asking."

"You're welcome. Talk to you later, Paul."

"Ok."

After going through a mental tug of war, he is more confident as each minute passes.
Now it's time to focus on his mission because one mistake could land him in jail or worse, death! Now Paul have to put his bathroom carts away and

get ready.

Paul opened his closet door
and hung his toiletries keys
on a shelf and took a spin
around to look at his closet
as if it was his last time
seeing it, or his last time
seeing it like a reasonable
person. He sighed hard,
then cut the light out and
closed the door. Paul
headed to the elevator on
the sixth floor, pressed the
button and waited.

After a minute and a half, it

showed up, and he got on and pressed the first-floor button. The door closed, then the elevator moved. "BING" someone on the fifth floor needed to get on, Paul thought to himself, *Okay*, as the co-worker got in. Seconds later the door closed then they were back in motion "BING" fourth floor. Paul got more irritated as the next co-worker got in. Then Paul sighed and rolled his eyes at each level as the car got slower and Fuller.

"BING" third floor. Paul thought *Really? Fuck*!!! Paul stormed out of the elevator and ran to the stairwell. *Shit, I bet I could beat them down to the first floor. Said, Paul,* as he hurried down the stairs on a contestant in a weight loss contest. He panted like he was out of shape and almost stumbled but he regained his balance to keep moving. Paul was on a mission that he had to mentally, physically and psychologically prep himself for.

These thoughts danced around in his head since his inner demons told him to start tonight. Paul took the stairwell to the lower level to go straight out the building to his car got the bags out of the trunk first, and then he got in the back seat to get organized. Ok, where are the dresses? Nope, not this sack, hardware supplies. Ok, the robes and wig. Good thing Paul had a two-door hatchback so no one could see him change. Paul laid the clothes on the driver's seat because there was very little room in the back seat

Everything was well planned cause his wife uses the car on weekends, so she leaves supplies in the car. Shoes, makeup, and razors. Paul took his shirt off, then his shoes, and he slid off his jeans, then threw them on the floor.

He sat there for five

minutes thinking of becoming a woman and earning the trust of horny men. The latter part should be the easiest cause it doesn't take much to get a man horny and when lust is involved, they let their guard down. A piece of Cake!

Paul was turned on as he slid on the dress. The fabric of the dress rubbed across his nipples and gave him a spark of excitement. Then he put on the stockings. He

never had much body hair.
Then he pulled out a mirror
that was in his wife's bag
and started applying
makeup. Most men would
let the devil in their house
if she had a great pair of
tits, and they'll sell their
soul for a piece of ass. Paul
finished his face and
grabbed his wig and placed
it on his head, then looked
in the mirror.

Damn, I look good, then
laughed hard, then grabbed
his cell phone to pick who

his first victim was. Eddie works for the energy company, Ted the parcel service, Clark the postman or Thomas, the cable guy. Let me see, I'm going to send out a mass text, then figure out who's the first according to their schedules.

"Hey, it's Stacey. I changed my number. Let me know if you're available tonight because my husband is on vacation and I need a big dick."

Paul sat in the back seat humming Orgasm Addict by the Buzz Cocks. *He's an orgasm addict, He's always at it, He's an orgasm addict is still at it.* Buzz, oh a text back observed Paul. He grabbed the phone it was Stacey,

"Hey what time are you getting home? I need the car!!"

Paul ignored Stacey text and kept on waiting. Then

another message came in,
damn Stacey again,
"HELLO, Dumb Fucker
Text Me Back!!!" he said
nothing and sent nothing
back. It pissed him off
more and tempted him to
get her tonight, but that's in
the plans for later. Buzz,
Buzz. *Shit, I wish that
stupid bitch stops it before I
get her tonight and sell her
to the butcher for beer
money.*

Oh, it's Ted, "I wish I could
hang out with you, but my

niece is in town staying
with me. Shit, maybe when
she falls asleep. I'll text
you back when the coast is
clear."

"Ok," Paul texted back.
Send. Paul thought to
himself, *could he kill near
a child for them to find
their uncle dead? It would
be very traumatic and
wrong, but "the media"
messes up kids heads
altogether, making them
into little insecure ticking
time bombs, you're not thir*

enough, you don't have a six-pack, you're ugly, and you're not the right color. And that's just the reality shows, which isn't real Paul thought to himself.

Buzz Buzz, two text messages, a response from Ted and one from Clark. Ted: "Ok, I'll keep you posted!!!"

Paul responded: "XOXO." Send.

He then opened Clark's

message: "Who's this again?"

Paul responded: *It's Stacey. My old number was 651-277-01**. We fucked on your mail route multiple times. Cedar St?*" Send.

Buzz, Buzz. Another message: From Stacey: "Fuck it! I'll call a taxi, and I took money out of your drawer to pay for it. LOL."

"*That Bitch*," Paul yelled.

Buzz, Buzz. Thomas: "Hey,

I get off at 11 pm. I'll be ok after that.   My address is 4233 Blackbird Street apartment #421."

"Ok see you then," Paul responded. Send.

Buzz, Buzz. *Damn my phone is on fire tonight. Good thing it's a pay as you go phone.*

Buzz. Eddie: "Hey I wish I could hook up, but I'm pulling a double shift tonight. I'm free tomorrow.

Keep me in mind.

Paul responded: *"Ok, I will. See you tomorrow."* Send.

Buzz, Buzz. Paul, still sitting in the back seat, checked the next message. Oh, it's from Clark: "Hey, I'm good to go now shit!! I have to be at work at 5:00 AM so let me know?"

Paul responded: *"Ok give me your address, and I'll head straight on over."* Send.

Damn, Paul thought, two

victims tonight, what a streak. I knew buying four dresses would pay off! He laughed as he checked to make sure everything was together before he got the next text. *Latex gloves – check; shoe covers – check; glasses – check; box cutter – check; pitchfork – check; and chloroform - check.*

Buzz, Buzz. *Damn, thought Paul, I hope I don't forget something.* Clark: "Hey my address is 1010 Como Blvd East. It's a greenhouse. Just

ring the bell, and I'll be
ready."

Paul responded: *"Ok, give
me fifteen minutes, and I'll
be there."* Send

*Ok, let me get in the front
seat so I can head that way*
thought Paul. He got his
keys and looked in his
mirror.
Then put on his shoe covers
and started the car. Paul
noticed it began to rain.
Was this a sign from the
gods to not go through with

it or a sign to start his reign against the Wicked?

Well, either way, he had to start a means to someone's end. Trust was no longer granted on this planet, like an expired coupon, but death is always there with its arms ready to hug, from a businessman to a bug. Paul entered his car a good man but will leave his car a murderous woman.

As Paul puts his car in drive and pulls off, he

leaves behind a piece of himself, a weaker part, a part of him, he should have killed off a long time ago. As he gets closer and closer to Clark's house, his heart beats faster and faster, and the will to throw up isn't out of the question. He even pulls over before reaching his destination his nerves are jumping over the moon, but he must pull it together to pull this off.

Now two blocks away and take a deep breath to calm.

Now Paul pulls in front of
the chosen first house. Paul
scopes the area out before
leaving the car.
Everything's calm.
Except for a lady walking
her dog. Paul waits until
she's off the block.
Then comes another person
with a bag of groceries
walking on the other side of
the street. *"Fuck!!!*
I should kill everyone on
the block," Paul blurted
low. Then the guy walked
up the stairs. Paul thought
he should drive around to

the alley behind Clark's house and then text him, so he could enter that way and besides its dark back there. Perfect!

Paul: *"I'm in the back."* Send. Paul got out the car with his supplies in a bag and walked up the back stairs. Tap, tap at the back door.

Clark said from a distance, "One second."

"Okay," said Paul in his

light voice.

Then Paul reached into his bag for the chloroform, opened it up, poured some on a rag, then screwed the top back on and waited. After five seconds the door opened. Paul went inside and hugged Clark with one arm then cuffed the rag over his face. Clark dropped like a fly after being sprayed with raid. Paul turned around and closed the door. Paul looked at Clark and said

"look at him. He's sleeping.
He will not wake again."

Paul went into his bag, took
out a knife and jabbed it
into Clark's chest, but his
first strike didn't even
break his skin.
Then Paul thought of all the
pain Clark, and others have
brought to his life. He got
the gall to add more force,
so he stuck Clark again
through the neck, piercing
the floor. Blood sprayed
everywhere, like a miser
spitting out red paint.

"*Shit*!" said Paul as he panicked about the colossal mess. *Fuck*

Paul didn't know what to do, but he remembered as a child, being told, "Clean-up the messes you and your family make!" He thought first dispose of *The Trash*. In Paul's mind, anyone who cheats or helps someone too is Trash. Time was a factor. He dragged the body into the tub so he could pour sulfuric acid over the body and trash the remains.

Paul then had to clean the kitchen. He used oxy cleaner with a sponge and mop, so he won't track the blood out of the house. Using Oxy breaks up the blood residue, so the cleanup was quick!

After 20 minutes the kitchen was cleaner than before he had arrived. Paul went outside to the trunk, and pulled out the five-gallon jug of acid and ran back into the house. He went into the bathroom to pour the acid over the deceased and notice the big mess in the bathroom, two blood trails, and blotches. While the acid disintegrated Clark, Paul worked on the bathroom floor. After an hour, Paul had bagged up everything and had locked up the place where Clark lived and died. Paul made deposits in garbage trash cans throughout the city. "I hope Stacey's retched snatch was worth it Dude."

Buzz Buzz

Chapter 9:

Eating off the Plate of Hate.

Larry and Jolene met in high school and married soon after, just as Paul and Stacey had done. Larry and Jolene lucked out by meeting Benjamin when they were scrounging for work to make ends meet. Ben owns a cleaning company along and his wife, Mary. Then they added staff to expand the business until they were cleaning and maintaining over twenty buildings.

Jolene and Larry are Ben's favorite

because of their ability to work hard and cheap, so he made them supervisors, then part owners. Ben always paid his workers minimum wage and then lower if they Couldn't speak English. Jolene and Larry carried on the tradition. This practice enabled them to cut costs and boost profits under state contracts. As a result, they could go on five extravagant vacations per year.

Their management philosophy was to weed out the strong by riding them and making them quit and to keep the meek so they could have control and the loyalty.

No raises were given unless the workers were white or the national minimum wage increased, so they had to comply, but they complained about it. Damn! I don't want to pay those wetbacks and niggers one cent more," bitched Jolene, but Larry explained that they're paying for our home and vacations, then she understood.

Larry serves as a referee when his wife flies off the handle. She has got beaten up and had death threats because of her mouth. Around the workers, there were constant rumors about Jolene being a racist bitch.

Jolene is a boney forty-five-year-old who looks sixty due to excessive smoking, drugs, and alcohol, but in her head, she's hot and wanted by all the guys. In the summer, she gets paranoid and feels that women shouldn't dress in shorts, miniskirts and tank tops, but she does it and looks ridiculous. "Do as I say, not as I do."

Jolene is out of touch with her staff. As hated as she is, she feels she's a cool boss, the best boss anyone could ever have. Most bosses have their fair share of enemies, but Jolene has more than most!

Thomas: "off work and heading home." I have to jump in the shower, and I'll be ready for you, so come by in thirty minutes."

Paul: "No problem. I can wait."
Send.

Paul pulled into a dark alley, took off the blood-soaked dress and stuffed it in a bag, slid the stockings off and then the shoe covers. Then tied the top of the bag into a knot then sat it on the floor to burn later. Paul had covered his seats with towels beforehand to keep any blood residue from his car seats. Paul jumped into the backseat again to get ready for Tom. As Paul put on another dress, Buzz, Buzz. Paul checked his phone. *"Oh, fuck."*

Stacey: "Where the fuck are you? You haven't answered any of my messages."

Paul: "I'll be home soon." Send.

Paul finished getting dressed and *looked "Shit, its two past eleven and I haven't even put on my shoe covers yet.* As he was slipping on the first shoe cover, Buzz Buzz. *Oh, shoot. If I didn't need the phone, I'd kill the phone. Ugh!!! Time is riding my ass like these stockings. Got to give women credit when it's due. Don't know how they can wear this and walk in heeled shoes. Whew, good thing I'm not wearing those, I could have tripped and fell and been someone's bitch for the night. Oh, it's Tom."*

Tom: "Hey my little cum slut comes and get daddy's big dick. I'll be waiting with the door unlocked naked and hard for you."

Paul: "Ok. I'll be there in ten

minutes. Get ready, and I'll fuck you so good, you'll never recover, lover." Send.

Paul jumped back into the driver seat with a crooked wig, looked in the mirror and said to himself, *"After a fucked-up childhood, I knew my head would never be straight again."* He drove off more confident and relaxed than earlier, but as those who perform on stage know you must be little nervous.

Paul arrived at Tom's at eleven twenty and notice all the lights were on in his home. *He texted Tom to kill the lights because she's a*

married woman and don't want to
be caught, and for him to get in bed
and wait for her.

He reached for the door handle and froze to check the streets for any wandering pedestrians. Even past eleven, you can run into the "Oh I need some fresh air" asshole not realizing they could just open their window. Here we go again." As Paul headed up the stairs then letting himself in.

He dabbed the chloroform on the cloth and entered the bedroom. But to Paul's surprise there where three guys standing there naked. Paul had to think fast or get caught in a corn hold or get killed for being a cross-dresser, so he tried greeting each one with a hug. (Paul knew to drop the tallest guy out the bunch first) Then the other two ran like little bitches. So, the chase was on.

As a child, Paul's favorite place to hide was the closet. He flung the door open, found one inside and kicked him in the balls. As he bent over to grab his bruised jewels, Paul cuffed his face then he collapsed, descending into his last dream. He ran to find the remainder piggy, which was easy 'Because he was scared on the toilet. So Paul had compassion and told him to *finish. In his head, he thought, "I don't want to clean up two messes."* After he flushed Paul knocked him out and dragged him to the bedroom with the others.

As he pondered what to do, he glanced around the room. He looked at the photos of Tom and his family *"So sad when you get caught up in a web of deceit for a piece of ass that belongs to someone else,"* said Paul.

So Paul came up with a murder-suicide scenario to explain the triple murder scene: *Tom caught his boyfriend with another man and killed the both of them and then himself.* Paul searched the home for a plausible weapon while the three were still out cold. He thought, *"Knives? Nah. Let me check the closet for a gun."* As usual, in a shoebox above the hanging clothes was a Berretta. *"No wonder they're so many accidental shootings, but in this case   thanks to the easy find Tom."'*

Paul sat the gun down and went through Tom's dresser drawers, he found Socks, T-shirts, and Underwear. Then he came across one drawer with tons of condoms and underneath was sex toys. *"Hey, this is so perfect for the story,"* thought Paul. *"What's next? Set up the scene for murder."* *Paul placed the guys in place.*

"Everything has to be on point!! One mistake and the cops will be on my ass, and we don't need that. Paul sifted through the sex toys and said, *"GROSS!!! Good thing I'm wearing rubber gloves. Bingo! A big pink dildo. Let's put a condom on it so it can be safe.* After Paul put the condom on the toy he rammed it in Tom's ass then took it out, peeled the condom off then put the condom on the guy closest to

and said damn I'm so clever "Then
Paul laid the guy on his stomach on
top of Tom.

Then he put clothes on the third
guy. He placed the gun in his hand
for the prints. Paul then wrote the
letter:

To whom it may concern,
I am sorry for the pain I
caused, but my anxiety of Loss
love
is more significant than I
could bear.
How Could anyone live
with love betrayal? Sorry,
Mom and Dad. Please
understand and forgive

Me as I exit the earth. I Love
You,
Farewell.

Paul slid the pen in his hand, then
put it back on the dresser, stood the
guy up, placed the gun in his hand
and used his finger to pull the
trigger. Bang, bang delivering lethal
shots to Tom and the other guy.
Then Paul turned him. Then used
his finger to provide, the suicide
shot. Bang. Paul, then let him fall to
the ground and jetted out of the
house before anyone saw anything
Paul jumped into the car, sped off
and looked back

Then He heard sirens as he left the neighborhood. *"Whew, that was close."* Said, Paul, minutes later he pulled up In front of his house, He jumped into the back seat to change his clothes. He stuffed the dress, gloves and shoe covers into the plastic bag.

Then walked around to the back of the house to place the evidence into the trash can then splashed it with lighter fluid, then up in flames, it went, suddenly Stacey yelled, Where and the hell have you been? did you get any of my texts?"

Paul said nothing as he used the

water hose. Must be another woman," said Stacey.

"Like she can talk about infidelity!" Thought Paul. Then came into the house, kicked off his shoes, disrobed and then jumped into the shower.

He needed to unwind and rest after such a busy day. As he was putting on his pajamas, there was a loud knock on the bathroom door. Paul's heart started beating fast, not knowing who it was. "Was it the Police? Or just Stacey or her Fuck buddy?"

Paul replied in the wimpiest tone, *"Yes?"*

It was Ross, how much longer are you going to be Joe?
"It's Paul! My name is Paul, motherfucker and when I'm out you'll know!"

"Whatever," said Ross from a distance.

Knock knock. "Hey, you should ask people 'do they have to use the bathroom' before you get into shower!" lectured Stacey. Paul flung the door open, aiming to hit her with it. "Hey, fucker," as she leaped out of the way.

Are you ready to meet the maker?
Said, Paul

"Huh? What is that supposed to mean?" She asked

Paul ignored her as he went to the laundry room to put his dirties in the hamper. Ross entered the bathroom and she followed Paul to irritate him.

"Hey, you owe me an apology," said Stacey.

Huh? Said, Paul

"For being so strange lately and for being rude to our guest."

"Hmm," said Paul. "No! That's your guest, not mine". You didn't even ask me for permission to have a guest. But that's in your nature of being a dominant whore - forget how everyone else feels.   No more will you rule this nest.
No more!"

"What? Said Stacey.
Paul interrupted her, *"You know what you did by inviting someone into our mess of a home, our mess of a marriage. You etched the names*

on the graves of innocents before
the stones have even been
purchased."

"What? Speak English," she said.

"I'll show you later," said Paul.

"What will you show me, your little
Peter?" said Stacey

"Ok your very funny. Ha. We will
see how much you will be laughing
later," Paul said with a smirk. "I'm
going to bed. Go talk to your buddy
if you need someone to bitch at.
"Limp Loser" whispered Stacey.
Paul took off his slippers, fluffed his

pillow, and laid down and drifted off to dreamland. He ended up in a dark place of pain and regret, as he saw his victims asking him "Why did you kill us"? Paul answered tearfully, *"You defiled my marriage and the only punishment is death. The only punishment is death."* Over and over this statement was echoed in his dream 'till he woke up in a cold sweat by Stacey.

"Shut the fuck up," demanded Stacey.

"Huh?" Paul responded, still half asleep.

"You were talking in your sleep and

woke me up," Stacey complained.

Ring Ring Ring. "Ah, hello," said George.

"Georgie, oh my son, are you ok?"

"Mom, it's three thirty in the morning. Can this wait?"

"It's started."

"What?"

"The carnage, the darkness, and the deaths."

"Mom, I need the number to your doctor in the morning."

"Not a joke. It has started. Be careful. Be careful, My only son." Click.

"Hello, mom, hello. Ah, she needs her meds bad, back to bed I go. Ah, shit, let me drain the hose." George stumbled to the bathroom, took a piss and washed his hands. George rubbed his eyes as he looked in the mirror and he saw dark clouds and then bodies covered in blood then the mirror cleared up, and he screamed as if he was living in a nightmare. "Maybe I need meds, or

I need to stop watching horror movies before bed." He yawned and scratched his head then returned to bed.

George was slowly awakened by the breaking local news.

Field Reporter:

"Well, Bob, at 11:40 PM last night neighbors heard gunfire in this house behind me. Multiple shots rang out and woke this quiet part of town out of its sleep. The details are a little sketchy, but all we know now is there were three victims, two are dead, and one is in intensive care with a bullet lodged in his head. Investigators found a suicide note. The police aren't releasing the contents of the note or the names of the victims. A press conference is scheduled at noon today. Officials should be able to shine some light on the madness that rocked this small town last night."

Newscaster: "Thanks, Jeff."

Field Reporter: "No problem, Bob. Back to you."

Newscaster: "If you're just tuning in, there was a shooting last night…"

Click.

"Today on Jerry Springer, Cross-dressers' secrets."

Chapter 10:

Work Is Murder

Paul started the day in a regretful mood. He wore the word glum as if it was a suit while his feet dragged as if he was walking in a foot of snow. Bottom lip extended, 'the saddest movie ever' portrayed, *"I'm done with killing,"* he said to himself. *"I shouldn't have done it. Damn, I was wrong."* Paul got into the shower knowing that he must go to work. Fifteen minutes later while he was drying off, another loud knock that pissed him off.

Paul screamed, *"I'm tired of this shit!!! I can't take a fucking shower uninterrupted in my own home Damn!!*

"What did I tell you dick-less fucker? To let people, know before you get in the shower," yelled Stacey.

I don't need to let nobody know shit. I can do what the fuck I want when I want "Got that Bitch?" said Paul.

There was no response for ten seconds, then suddenly there was a loud thud at the door, and it flew open. "Don't you ever call me a bitch," screamed Stacey. Then she started to hit Paul, so he had to block the hit. Just when his towel fell, her friend came to help her. They both looked at Paul and starting at laughing at him.

"Damn is that a penis?" said Ross.

Stacey Fell on the floor laughing, "No, that's a big clit." More laughter roared louder.

Paul grabbed his towel to cover his privates. Ashamed, hurt and embarrassed, he ran to the bedroom and started Crying and fussing with himself. *"Hate her. Hate everybody. Sick of this shit. I wish had a button attached to a nuclear bomb. I would murder the world. Fuck everybody. Fuck them. I*

wish I wasn't born in such
a fucked up cruel world. No
love, just hate here, no
light, just darkness, the
pain I'm about to inflict
will keep people hiding
scared under their beds for
days," Paul whispered.
That remorse that plagued
him earlier went straight
out the window for
destruction and madness.

Paul got dressed and
headed for the door.
His eyes cut to his wife and

Ross who had smirks on their faces. *"Death is too easy for you,"* said, Paul, as he opens the door and then said, *"Your exit will be slow and painful."*

As Paul stormed out, he slammed the door so hard the glass fixtures shattered and didn't ponder. Then jumped in the car and took off without caution or care. He had so much emotion pumping through his blood, he shouldn't have been driving, but they say that drunk people shouldn't get behind the wheel, they still do. As Paul flew through traffic.

He mumbled, *"That stupid bitch. Always finds a way of making me feel like shit, similar to my fucked up family. They must have given her the blueprint for my degradation before we got married."*

Despite his negative feelings toward his family Paul still sometimes

wondered how his family
was doing. Does he have
any nieces or nephews and
if he does, do they even
know of their uncle, Paul?
It makes him sometimes
sad when his mind ponders
on the sentimental side.

Chirp, chirp. "PULL OVER
NOW,"
Blared from the police
vehicle. Paul was going
way above the speed limit
and didn't realize it.

"Fuck!!! You see nothing ever goes right for me" Paul yelled in his car as he pulls over. His heart pounding faster, and harder and while he thought, *"Why and the hell are they pulling me over?" for murder? Or Speeding? Or a quota ticket for a first-row seat at the policeman's ball?"*

One of The officers got out of the vehicle, as his partner sat watching for any risky movement from the

perpetrator in question.
With his hand on his gun,
the officer got to the
window and asked,
"LICENSE AND
REGISTRATION."

Paul mumbled as he
reached for the items in
question.
"NOW KEEP YOUR
HANDS ON THE
WHEEL, SIR," said the
officer.

*"Do you want my proof of
fucking insurance too?*

Geez," said Paul.

"Sir, I didn't curse at you. So please give me the respect I gave you."

"I'll be back in a few," said the officer as he headed back to the squad car to run Paul's information on the computer.

"I hate to be late," said Paul, looking at his watch and thinking of his boss.

Paul turned on the radio to

calm his nerves, and then he heard the news, *WHAT'S GOING ON IN ST PAUL?* "With a rash of crimes including unsolved murders, robberies, and rapes…"

"Wow," "I better move from the cities soon before I become a statistic." Said Paul then chuckles.

The 2nd Officer tells his partner, "That's my numb nut of a brother, Paul. OH, I have a plan. "Let's mess with him." The other officer agrees as he leans in to hear the plot. "Ok, let's make him believe that he's wanted for murder and make him get on the ground and stuff you know the full routine."

"Ha, you're mean," laughed the 2nd Officer.
Hey, I had years of training of being a shit-head, replied the 1st Officer.

Paul looked in the mirror and saw the officers getting

out the vehicle with their guns drawn. *"Oh, shit,"* said Paul and thought, *"maybe they're rescuing me from killing anymore, but I won't say anything till it's time."*

"GET OUT THE CAR!"

Paul cowered out of the vehicle with his hands up. *"Don't shoot,"* he screamed.

"GET ON THE GROUND NOW!" He fell into the

fetal position. "ON YOUR STOMACH WITH YOUR LEGS AND ARMS SPREAD."

"Oh, ok officer sirs," said Paul.

Then Paul's brother put his knee on Paul's back as he grabbed his hands to cuff him. Click Click,

"Why am I," Paul began to protest

"SHUT YOUR MOUTH,

MAGGOT, AND
LISTEN."

"Ok," responded Paul.

"YOU'RE A SUSPECT IN
A MURDER
INVESTIGATION SO
CHOOSE YOUR WORDS
CAREFULLY BECAUSE
THEY MIGHT
INCRIMINATE YOU IN A
COURT OF LAW."

"Wait a minute," Paul said
to himself. *"I know that
voice. That's my brother.*

What? A cop? Oh shit! Damn!"

"Get up." Oops, you can't. Let me help you up bro, damn you packed on pounds. Is Stacey feeding you good?" Paul's brother inquired.

"Nope," replied Paul. *"Aside from being the town slag, she's not a good cook unless it's smoking someone else's sausage."*

"Ha, damn, I didn't know

you were so funny Paul,"
said his brother.

*"Yeah, my life is one big
recurring joke,"* said Paul.

"Sorry for the prank," said
Paul's brother.

"Me too," said the other
officer.

Click, click. "You're free to
go, bro. Hey, what's your
cell number so I can keep
in touch with you?" asked
Paul's brother.

Paul replied, *"I'll put it on your cell phone.* Seven beeps later and he was back on the road. Relieved and soaked for pissing his pants.

Since he works in the bathroom, no one should notice the smell, and besides, he can shower there after work so he can finish the task."

Before he walked into work, Paul remembered

putting an extra shirt in the trunk last week so he could wrap around his waist to cover the spot until it dried. With one minute to spare, until the bitching hour. Paul ran into the building and bumped into a lady leaving.

"Damn," she said. "Watch where you're going, you dirty, stinky, bastard." Giggles from her friend as they exited the building. Paul looked them up and down and gave them the stink eye.

He signed in and started work. Paul whisked through his shift as a chef would. No nerves or reserves for Paul as he finished.

"Hey, Paul."

"Hey, George. Whew, you almost gave me a heart attack," said Paul.

"Sorry, man. I didn't mean to," said George.

"It's ok I'm a little too

focused sometimes, what's up?" replied Paul.

"Well, Jolene wanted me to ask you are you willing…" began George.

"I can't. I can't. Not tonight. Maybe tomorrow," in a defensive tone said Paul?

"Whoa, slow Up, Paul. I'm just asking. Well, you know how she is. You know how she gets when she can't get her way. She turns into a

mega bitch. Ah, I
sometimes think of Kill…
Oh, never mind," explained
George.

*"It's no problem, you're
just the messenger,"* said
Paul.

"Yeah, I know. Jolene
irritate all of us sometimes,
probably Even Larry, I bet
he wants to get a muzzle
for that …." replied
George.

"You see, brighter things in

life comes from a few sentences when you don't have to go home with her," said George. Then laughter broke out between the two. "I'll let her know you have plans."

"Oh, ok. Thanks," said Paul.

As George turned away, Paul headed to put away his carts. Then he catches the elevator to the sixth floor and around the corner, POW! Larry and Jolene stood in front of his closet.

"Hi Paul," said Larry.

"HI, " replied Paul.

"Do you want to keep working here!?" asked Jolene.

"yes, " Paul responded. "What's going on? They questioned, and I answered *I'm busy tonight.*

"Well, we really need you

tonight," Stated Larry. "And we are willing to give you two extra hours pay."

"We should just fire his ass," said Jolene. "How dare he deny and act selfishly to us after all that we did for him?"

Hush dear, "honey and flies, honey and flies," said Larry.

"But, but ..." sputtered Jolene.

"Hush," cautioned Larry.

"I guess, I can. I can cancel my plans," Paul replied.

"Thanks, Paul. I appreciate it," Larry said.

"No problem," said Paul, with a smile on the outside while screaming on the inside as he was thinking of a variable to his plans for tonight.

"We'll meet you in the

lobby for the instructions," said Larry.

"Ok, I'll be right down, " said Paul.

Then he continued putting his cart away, hearing her talking more shit in the distance. Paul said in his low tone, *"I need to put her on the list!! This is the last time I'm doing extra's for them!"*

The elevator opens. Outcomes Paul. "Well, I'm glad you made it," said

George.

Paul was mute as his eyes
rolled in his head.

"Well, two people didn't
show up in the other
building, so we have to
clean a set of bathrooms
and two floors which one
person had the duties of.
Let's get in my truck, so we
knock this out people,"
instructed Larry.

"Ok, alright, ok," said the
Janitors. Everyone piled
into the boss's SUV. "Wow,
I wish I could get one of

these," thoughts ran
through the helpers' minds,
as 70's classic rock blasted
in the ears of everyone.

Paul's head sank to his
chest as he thought, *"There
must be a God because he
saved someone's ass
tonight."*

"Ok, we're here guys,"
Larry informed the crew.
Everyone emptied out of
the vehicle and stood to
face Larry. "Paul, you got
the bathrooms. George and

Nate, you got one of the
two floors decide who will
vacuum or trash and me
and Jolene will knock out
the rest.

"Let's hurry so we can get
out of here within an hour,"
Paul said.   *"These aren't*
my bathrooms so fuck it,
and I'll half-ass it. If we get
out of here quick enough,
who knows, the devil could
win and bowl the two souls
to hell."

Paul Text Ted, "What time
you want to hook up?
XOXO Stacey." Send.

Paul shoved the phone back into his pocket then grabbed the mop to finish the fifth floor Men's bathroom.

"Beep Beep," Ted responded. "After 10, because I need your pussy bad!!"

Paul messaged back, "Ok, I need some big dick. After 10 is cool. I'll text you later to get your address. Later." Send.

At 9:05 Paul finished up the bathrooms - six sets in 30 minutes, a record in janitorial history!

"Hey, you're done?" asked Larry.

"Yep," Paul responded.

"Well help me finish trashing," Asked Larry.

"Ok," said Paul.

They were done in five

minutes. "Thanks, Paul. You are one of the best we have. Sorry that my wife gives you guff, but she gives me guff at home, a lot!" Paul smiles before they both chuckled.

Minutes later they piled into the vehicle and headed back to the main building. Paul had his eyes on his watch, "Come on, and playing over and over in his mind as his eyes watched the time tick by.

"Beep Beep," Ted message,
"112 Beech Street sweetie.
Fucking you soon."

"Ok Hun can you dim your
lights at your place because
you know I'm married,
XOXO, Stacey." Send.

Paul crawled into the back
seat to put on his costume
as time ticked. Then he was
on his way. This time
around was calmer than
usual, Paul was becoming a
pro. Who knows, he could

be the next Bundy or
Speck. Paul hates
comparisons or
competition, He just likes
doing a good job.

"Beep Beep. Ok, will do,"
from Ted.

*As Paul made his journey
he pondered should he use
a knife or a gun? I guess
we'll make it up as we go
along.* "

Paul headed down Beech
Street and noticed how dark

and deserted this block was
had no street lights. Paul
said *"PERFECT!"* As he
pulled in front of Ted's
house and messaged "I'm
here." Send.

Paul gathered his bag and
headed up the stairs,
"Knock, knock." The door
creaked open, *"Hey,
honey,"* then Paul knocked
Ted out cold with one
punch.

Paul figured *Since Ted was
shorter put him in the*

trunk. So, he did.

And got into the driver seat
then closed the door.
*"Hey, let's make it an
accidental drowning in the
closest pond."* Thought
Paul. He Drove backward's
to the shore and got out,
opened the trunk and slid
Ted out. Paul looked at
Ted's unconscious form
and thought, *"will drown
before he awakes."* Then
pushed Ted into the water.
He sank into the muddy
lake full of sludge as the air

escapes from his lungs making a bubbling sound as if you were pushing air through a straw while drinking a milkshake. After scanning his circumference out of his peripheral, he got back in the car and drove away.

As Paul left the lake, he asked himself, *"Can we go for one more?" Sure, let's finish up the list! Let's see if Eddie's niece is still staying with him.*

"Hey, it's Stacey. Do you
still have company?" Send.

Paul cruised the streets and
waited for a response with a
crooked wig and all. Then
after 10 minutes had
passed, he said, *"Fuck it
I'm going home.*

One block away from the
house he pulled over to
change his clothes.
After a big sigh of relief
from being so tired, Paul
pulled the wig off his head

and jumped in the back
seat.

"Beep Beep."

*"What the Fu..... It's too
bad. I'm not changing
back,"* said Paul as he
grabbed the phone.

"Hey, Stacey my niece
leaves tomorrow afternoon,
so I'll be free after that,"
Said Eddie.

"Ok, that sounds good."
Texted Paul AKA Stacey

Paul finished getting
dressed before entering the
house because he couldn't
explain wearing woman
clothes and makeup. He
could hear her now, "Oh
that explains everything,
my lack of lust for you and
how horrible you are in bed
and I knew sex with you
felt funny, and I'm not a
lesbian, dammit!!"

He pulled up in front of the
house, got out of the car,
grabbed the mail out the

box and headed in. He
noticed as he looked to his
Left, Stacey sitting on Ross
lap on the couch and Paul
said *(Okay)* then he walked
into the kitchen.

Looked in the fridge,
nothing was appealing to
him, yawned and thought, *I
can go days without eating,
a trait I picked up living
with my loving family.* Then
he went to the Bedroom.

Paul got into his pajamas
and laid down, hoping to
fall asleep fast, but he

couldn't. He was tossing and turning: lumpy mattress, loud TV. Laughter and giggling turned to whispers then moaning, as Paul was drifting away to sleep saying, *"I should be moaning and fucking, I should be Zzzzzzzzzzzz."* Paul fell asleep with sex on his mind with the dream inspiration from the act that's going on in the living room.

He faded away from his house of broken vows and

broken dreams to a beautiful calm environment. Paul was on a beach enjoying the balmy weather and peace, lying in a lawn chair, sipping on a drink. Then he noticed one island girl flirting with him, so he winks at her. She smiled back. Then another one started winks at him, then another and another. Paul was wondering why gorgeous women were digging on him. Even in his dreams, he was a doubting Thomas. Then he found himself surrounded by island girls. Then all it took was for one of them to pull his shorts off, and Paul smiled and said, "It's on!"

The girls ravished him with kisses all over his body, while two were sucking, on each of his nipples, and two more were sucking on his cock and balls. Then one girl pushes them aside and got on top and Started Riding him hard and fast. Paul noticed there were at least twenty women around him. He closed his eyes in ecstasy and reopened them and then twice as many women were around him and saw his chair had moved.

Paul thought, "Maybe it's all the riding, pulling and attention." Then he closed his eyes again, this time for even longer. He smelled the salt water scent got stronger. When he opened his eyes again, he was two feet from the water and wondering what the hell

going on. But such a
deprived person didn't care
because he was getting
laid.

All the girls stopped
suddenly, then turned and
faced the ocean. Paul said,
"Hey what's wrong? Why
you stopped?"

Silence fell around him. It
got colder, and the sky got
dark like a storm was
coming. "Hey what
happened? Did someone
drown? Did someone get

hurt?

Nothing was said.
Paul looked around the
beach. "Hello," said Paul.
"Ladies, can you hear
me?"

Mute again. After a minute
of silence, Paul heard the
swooshing of water. Then
the heads of the ladies
turned to him, as if they
were owls, as their bodies
still faced the ocean. Paul
then noticed the faces of the
women where decayed and

*bloated as they had
drowned years ago.*

*The ladies started crying.
Paul tried scooting away,
not knowing what the next
move from the creepy
looking women was.
Something was coming out
of the water. It looked like a
Kraken. Then the ladies
grabbed him like he was a
Volley Ball or rock star
stage diving*

*Paul screamed as they
flung him near the*

Creature. Nothing happened. As he turned and crawled his way back to shore and was about to get up, it dragged him into the water.

"Help, help," as his body submerged into the water until his lungs filled with water. He thought he had a fighting chance, then "Gulp, gulp," ringing in ears, and then his heart stops... Then Paul awakes, taking deep breaths like he was having an asthma

attack, *"Damn ...."*

"Whew, shit! I hate nightmares." Paul got up to get a drink of water and noticed his wife lying on Ross on the couch, naked, with his dick protruding through her legs, as if they were sleeping spooning. Anger struck him, as a lightning rod to the Back.

Paul went into the kitchen and got the biggest butcher knife. He stood there for a second to think it through.

He then put it down and said, "Fuck it." But then Paul said to himself, *"Wait a minute. I'm in my territory." So,* He grabbed the knife and headed to the living room. Paul said, *"The Livingroom no more, It's the Death room."* One Stab to Stacey's chest woke her. Then she took another blow to the neck that punctured her vocal cord and out came the gush of blood. Ross was still sound to sleep till his penis head got severed. Then he got up screaming. Then Paul struck him in the temple that took him out. As Ross body flung back onto the couch, Paul was Giddy like a kid in a candy shop and said "Wow!! I got a major mess to clean up, but it can wait. As I said, 'I'm on my stomping ground.' I'm still tired. Let me wash my hands and take my butt back to sleep."

Paul got in bed, relieved
that one of his life monsters
is dead. His only worry is
having more nightmares, so
he decided to take a mild
sedative. Hopefully, this
will offset his elusive
dreams. Off he went to
Sandman's land. At 6:30 in
the morning, Paul's eyes
popped open, but this
wasn't a dream. Something
woke him up. His ears were
peeled listening for
anything strange. One

minute had passed and nothing, so Paul Whispered, *"Fuck it I'm going back to sleep.* Every hair stood up on Paul's body as a chill went up to his spine, *"Fuck, oh fuck. I thought I, Ah, killed. Shit!"* He shot out of bed and slowly peeked around the corner. He saw Ross with that frozen dead look lying in a puddle of blood, but no Stacey. *"Huh?"* Then, Paul felt a tug at his ankle. He looked down and saw his wife. She appeared so innocent looking up at him with tears in her eyes, looks that said she was sorry for mistreating him for so long. Paul wished that he hadn't wounded her so severely. As he looked at the wedding photo on the wall and missing the old days. He got kind of choked up with remorse, and a tear fell from his right eye and then looked over at Ross and snapped out of it and went to the kitchen to get a knife to put her out of her misery.

Chapter 11:

By the Way

Ring……….. Ring, "George are you there?" His Mom asked.

"Long yawn …..Yeah, I was sleeping. What time is it? Asked George.

11 am said, mom.

"Yawns again, are you sure? What's wrong now?" said George with a smirk of derision.

"Um, I know you are tired of me discussing your job,".

"Nah, I love hearing from you. It's just sometimes in the morning or at night, to hear stuff that's strange and

spooky is a little too much,"
explained George.

"I'm so sorry for my ramblings.
Someone's been sending me
messages, and I'm just warning
you. So, how's work?" She asked.

"It's ok, just cleaning behind slobs,"
said George.

"That's good,"
The reason for this call is I've been
watching the news. There has been
a spike in murders in Saint Paul
Mom explained.

, "Yeah, but the world is a
dangerous place..." responded
George

She didn't wait for him to finish.

"But some of the murders are

related to someone that you work with," "Okay"

"But George!!" "You've been dismissing my warnings, thinking that I'm old or my lack of Medicine," said Mom.

"Huh? What?" George questioned in surprise. I'm your Mother I gave birth to you, not your friends, listen "I have these new powers for a reason, and it's to warn you! He's killed and will continue, for instance, the murder-suicide, and the drowning Mom explained. George was all ears now in shock because the details his Mother had told him. She had now ruled the Conversation which he had always dismissed, and now he knew that he had to pay attention to save his life.

"Ok Georgie, I love you, be cautious and safe," Mom said.

"Love you too. And I'm sorry I didn't believe you before, said George.

"It's ok," replied Mom. I better get up and get ready for the day I'll talk to you later.

"Ok, son,"

"Bye, bye," Mom.

Rolled up in a beige rug lies, two Lovers, then placed in a Large plastic bag to contain the crimes and Carnage. The garage door opens, and Paul stands there waiting for the trash men to pull up to help him. And yes, Paul has a crisp hundred-dollar bill for the help to banish his problems. And here they come.

"Hey!! Hey! Over here!" Paul yelled.

"Yeah!!" the trash man hollered back.

"Hi. Could you guys help me for a sec?" asked Paul.

"Sure. Hey, that isn't bodies rolled up in that is it?" the trash guy inquired. Paul nearly shit his pants.

"I'm just pulling your chain," said

the trash man, "but it's going to cost you."

"No problem," said Paul. He watched as the guys tossed the bag into the truck and pressed the compressor. Then, deep inside, Paul went *"whew"* as he handed them a hundred dollar bill.

"Whoa, what a big tip! They laughed as they talked of pizza and a twelve pack of beer and then they left.

"Bye Stacey. Bye Ross," said Paul as he closed the garage door and went back inside, then screamed,

"Yeah! Yes! She's gone! Whew!"

Then Paul took the wedding picture off the wall and threw it in the trash.

Then Paul thought to himself, *"Who's going to help me with the bills now? Oh! She didn't pay any bills."*

"I think I should celebrate with a beer and an escort.

Paul thumbed through an older Neighborhood Pages and found a Lady named Amber: a 20-year-old redhead, 5 feet 4, 120 pounds, $150.00 Firm.

Paul circled her, then cleaned up around the house and brought Stacey's clothes down to the car.

"Man do I smell," time for a

shower said, Paul. Minutes later he got out and dried off and walked around the house in the buff and felt free and liberated then he grabbed his phone and called Amber.

Ring…Ring……. Click. "Hello," a young woman answered.

"Ah hi. This is Paul. I saw your ad on the Pages, and I wanted you for this afternoon if you can fit me in," said Paul.

"Oh yeah. I can fit you in real good, I can come now if you're ready," said Amber.

"Ok, now is great. I'm fresh and naked from the shower," replied Paul.

"Well, that sounds good. Where are you located? Asked Amber. Paul gave her his address and got ready. *Oh man! I'm about to get some, I should do push-ups even though I'm somewhat in shape, being a janitor and 'an exterminator,' you must be. Never heard of a fat killer unless it's liposuction.* Paul did three sets of twenty of each and was ready for Amber.

"Let me find some condoms and hope they're still good it's been so long. But, oh yeah, since she was the only active person in this house she should have a drawer full of

them, Fucking slag, she's probably screwing the devil in hell right now. Yep, just as I thought, a box and a half of rubbers.

DING DONG Paul smiled with the giddiness of people around Christmas time.

"Just a sec. I'm coming!!" Paul said just as he grabbed a bathrobe He peeked out the window and saw this lady wearing a one-piece tight red dress. His Face was flushed. *"I hope she doesn't want to talk because today I'm thinking about my cock."*

Paul opened the door with a smile and bulge. *"Come on in and have a seat. Would you like something to drink?*

"No thanks. I want to serve you," Amber replied.

"Ok, then let's start," said Paul.

"Money first," business before pleasure said Amber. No pun intended but I got screwed many times for my money.

"No problem $150.00, right?"

"Yes," said Amber.

Then Paul peeled off $200 from the role of money he had in his hand and said, *"Let get started,"* as he passed her the money.

Amber put it in her purse, then

stood up and the red dress dropped.

Paul said, *"Whoa, no panties or bra? Damn you're hot!"*

"Thanks. You too," replied Amber. Paul opened the condom packet then unrolled it on his unit. He bought Amber to the bedroom. She laid on the bed then opened her legs to accept Paul's loving. As he climbed on top, his body shook as he was nervous.

She kissed him on the shoulder and caressed his back to relax him and said, "It's ok. Give me that dick," and he smiled and exhaled then slid his penis into her vagina and started with small stokes to learn her body frame till he found his groove.

Amber started moaning, then Paul got a boost of confidence and sped up. Ten minutes later he turned Amber over to hit it from the back, then placed his hands on her waist and started beating her pussy up like he was a pro.

"Fuck me hard," she moaned.

Then Paul slapped her on the ass and said, *"Hell yeah,"* and sped up faster and faster. Amber was enjoying this, not that he had a ten-inch cock but watching and feeling him become more dominate turned her on, and she came two times since he started.

Then Paul stopped and switched positions again saying, *"I want you to ride me,"* so he lay on his back. "Ok baby," said Amber, panting and shocked. She got on top and started. Their eyes connected and she started digging on him in a 'no future charges to fuck' way.

Paul was moaning as she was in total control of him, then he grabbed the sides of the mattress to brace himself on the wild romp he was getting. Awe he was coming, and she kept riding to get every drop out of his balls.

"Fuck oh fuck! Whew!!" said Paul as she got off of him.

She looked at her watch and said to herself, "44 minutes, damn that was good!" Paul laid there to recoup for a sec before walking Amber to the door.

Paul rose, then put on his robe, walked into the living room and said, *"You were amazing. Damn!"* Amber was putting back on her dress and said, "You were too." Paul said, *Yeah, right.*

Amber said, "Yes you were. I came twice. I should be paying you and to show you how serious I am, I'm coming back tomorrow, and there will be no charge!"

Paul smiled and said, *"Thanks."*

Amber said, "Thank you. Here's my

personal cell number so you can call me. Then she kissed him on the cheek and grabbed his ass. "See you, tomorrow babe."

"Ok," said Paul. *"See you, Hun."*

Paul closed the door and shouted, *"Yeah!!! Whew!!!"*

Then Paul started singing *"I got some pussy, I got some pussy. Hey, that could be a hit song.* Then he got in the shower and kept singing. His mood has elevated so high that the astronauts couldn't reach it in a rocket. Paul was a single, married man living alone in a house that hate build, but the wicked witch was dead, and he was ready to play. *It's Friday and payday, and I feel good,"* Paul said to himself.

"Hey there's still one more on my list, well ....I'm done with that chapter of my life and Eddie should thank his niece because she saved his life."

Paul got dressed for work and knew he had forgotten something he needed to do. So he went to the car and gathered the props, took them to the backyard, dropped the bag in the can, sprayed them with lighter fluid, then poof.

People at work, including Jolene, felt the change in their gloomy co-worker, Paul.

"Hey Paul," said George.

"Hey, George. How are you?" Paul replied with a Smile.

"I'm doing well and you? Asked George with a strange look across his face

"I'm doing great," Paul responded.

"Hey boss lady, you don't need me for extra work tonight do you because my schedule is Clear," said Paul.

"Oh my God, the dead awakes and speaks," said Jolene. "I'll let you know if people call in."

"Ok thanks," said Paul, as he signed in.

Chirp "Yep," said Larry.

"Hi, let me know if you need my staff," Jolene said

"Ok why," asked Larry.

"Just because Paul told me he was free for the night."

"What?" said Larry?

"Yes, that's what I was thinking. Paul's wife must have given him some," said Jolene with laughter.

"Ok," said Larry.

"Thanks. Love you Hun" said Jolene.

Chirp "You too sweetie," responded Larry.

Jolene Chirped Stephen.

He replied, "Hey boss lady."

"Hey Stephen, could you come down to the first floor now? Jolene asked.

"Why?" responded Stephen. "I'm pouring acid in the toilets." "Just finish that set and get down here M.N.H.D." demanded Jolene. "Ok. Right away boss," Stephen replied.

Jolene speaks acronyms when she hangs around the security desk F.M.N =Fuck me now, and M.N.H.D =Mommy needs her dick and so on and so on. She should have been caught knowing her husband is just next door.

Not saying Larry is an angel. He finds his way to women. They look at him as a man of power and authority, and feel bad for him being married to Jolene!

Ring, Ring "Hi Jolene," said Nathan.
Jolene speaking and panting response, "Hi."

"I didn't mean to disturb you. This is Nate. I'm at the hospital with my mom. She fell and hit her head, and the doctor said it doesn't look good ……….. So I won't be in today."
"Well, you're ok! You can still come in," directed Jolene.

Silence fell for ten seconds.

Do you want to work here or not?"

said Jolene.   "You

caught me in the middle of

something, and I don't have time to

play on the phone!"

"I need my job.......I'll be in," said

softly Nathan.

"I thought so," said Jolene. Click.

Nate left the payphone and headed

back to his mom's room. "Mom,

I'm sorry I have to leave you and go

to work I don't have the nicest boss

in the world

Nate kissed his mom on the

forehead and told her he loves her

and will be back after work.

"Bye Mom"

He went to the receptionist, "Here's my cell number if the doctor needs to contact me."

The receptionist responded, "Ok will do."

"Thanks," said Nate and headed through the double doors to catch the next bus.

On the schedule he looked, "Cool three minutes to the next one."

But those three minutes felt like three hours because of the pain and sorrow of leaving his mom behind. Tears fell down his face. "I'm a bad son," he thought. Then the bus pulled up, and he got on. He didn't wipe his tears, so there were stares, but Nate didn't give a fuck his feelings were numb.

After fifteen minutes he got off the bus and dragged himself into work. Though he was late, he didn't care. After scanning his card, the guard asked him what's wrong.

Nate confided. "My mom is on her deathbed in the hospital, and I had to come in."

"Wow! Your boss is a heartless bitch!" the guard replied.

Nate nodded his head in agreement.

"Well, I'll pray for your mom," said the guard.

"Thanks," said Nate then got in the elevator to go to his assigned floor.

Put his jacket away in his work closet, got his trash can and started his work.

"Hey Paul," said George. "Sorry to disturb you."

"How can I help you?" said Paul. "Just wanted to say, 'what's up' you seem extra happy today. Just wanted to check on you," said George. *"I'm good, better than good. I would say 'great.' I had fantastic sex with my new friend,"* said Paul. "Oh, aren't you married Paul?" asked George.

Paul was caught off guard then

lowered his head and said, I lost my wife, and now I'm getting back into the dating scene, and she's Hot! Sorry that I got everyone riled up because I'm happy now." Sorry *for your loss said, George*

"Thanks," said Paul.

"Hey, maybe we can have a double date soon?""

"That sounds like a plan," said Paul.

"Ok," said George

Paul went back to cleaning the bathrooms as George walked to the elevator.

Ring... Ring went Paul's cell phone. *"Hello,"* Paul whispered.

"Hi honey," replied Amber.

"Hey, how is your day going?" Paul asked.

"It's ok. I haven't had any calls today, and my rent is going to be short this month," said Amber.

"Oh, sorry to hear that, maybe I can help out," Paul said.

"Awe, you're a sweetheart,"

"Ok, if it comes to that," said Amber.

Paul said *"I got your back even though we just met.*

I kinda dig you.

"You too," said Amber

"Thanks for digging me," said Paul.

Amber said, "I can give you a buzz

or stop by for a nightcap.", *"Either one is just fine. I'm not a fussy person nor a bug."* Paul said

"Well, I'll just have to surprise you, Hun. I'll talk to you later," Amber said.

"Ok later," Paul responded with an ear to ear grin.

Click then he put the phone back in his pocket and picked up his rag and stainless steel spray to finish polishing the sink chrome.

Ring......Ring

"Hello"
"Hi, may I speak to Nathan Smith?
"Hi, this is him."   "This is Nurse

Claire at the St John's hospital."

"Is my mother ok?"

"We need for you to come here as soon as you can."

"But is she ok?"

"I'm not able to talk about medical prognosis over the phone.

"Ok, I'll be finished here at work shortly."

"Ok, Nathan. Well, see you soon."

"Ok bye,"

All Nate needed to do was dust the other half of his floor, which takes ten minutes. He grabbed the duster and went through the work area as if he was riding a broomstick, not

missing an inch of dust anywhere.
Worried and sad, Nate kept his
composure. He knew what his boss
would say if he left early, but he'd
finish his job, and no one needs to
cover for him. Nate got out of the
elevator, hoping that Jolene was in a
better mood, so he can ask her to
leave early, but he was ready for
any response, and he would even
make the ultimate sacrifice for his
mom by quitting on the spot and
tighten his belt with dignity.

"Excuse me, I finished my floor
early so I can go check on my
mother at the hospital?" "I guess it's
ok. Hopefully, you did a good job,

I'll have George check your floor said, Jolene.

"Oh, thanks," said, Nathan, as he turned away to head to the door Shook his head in disbelief on how his boss treats her employee's. Jolene was daddy's little girl until he left home when she was ten years old. She was always optimistic that he would someday come back home, but why would he?

They argued daily over the - sex, money, and communication. Then one day all of a sudden, he had enough. Unlike the "I'm going to get some cigarettes cliché," he told his wife and daughter he was going

out to get some milk One-hour past.
"It doesn't take that long to get
milk," said Jolene's mom.

After not getting any sleep hoping
that every noise they heard was him
returning home to his girls, the
reality settled in and was daunting.
He was not coming back. Their
hearts were empty, not knowing
what had happened to him, was he
killed, kidnapped or just gave up on
us. Months had passed after the
missing person report, and life had
returned to normal minus one.

The bond between Jolene and her
mom was tight until she met Jack.
He was the crowbar in their door,

the wrench in their gears. He was 21 and Jolene was 16. Her mom was against it, as most parents would be, but inside Jolene always felt her mom drove her father away and developed the world owed her something attitude, The 'I- Me- Mine syndrome.' But when it came to Jack, she melted like butter in the frying pan.

Jolene's mom ranted, "You're too young for him.

"In rebuttal, Jolene shot back, "You don't understand, so think twice before giving out advice…. you couldn't keep your man"

This went on for months until that fateful week when Jolene and Jack came up with a plot to kill her mom. I'll set the house on fire while you are at school so you'll have no connection to the crime said Jack, as it was one of the schemes they were planning. Then one day Jolene came home in a mood from the night before getting into a fight with Jack about changing her mind over her mom.

The first thing she notices is the TV volume was loud, so she screamed, "Hey could you turn that shit down. I have a lot of freaking homework to do, so I need it quiet in here!!

Into her room, she entered. She
threw her backpack on the floor,
flopped on her bed then sighed then
rolled her eyes as if what she and
her mom were going to fight about
tonight. Jolene walked to the
kitchen to grab something to drink.
Got a cup out of the cupboard,
unscrewed the top to the juice bottle
and poured. She then screwed the
lid back on the bottle and placed it
back into the fridge then returned to
her room. Jolene closed her
bedroom door, laid on her bed and
cried as she stared at the ceiling, her
tears ran into her ears. She turned
over to her side and looked at the
phone. Swallowed her pride and

thought of calling Jack.

Grab the phone and placed the receiver to her ear, and heard nothing, no dial tone. So, she yelled, "Hang up the fucking phone." I'm trying to make a call."

"Damn she probably knocked it off the receiver," said Jolene   She got off the bed then walked to the door and opened it stuck her head out and yelled, "Hang up the phone! Hang it up!!" Then she went back to the phone and tried it again with no dial tone.

"Ok, fight number one is about to start," thought Jolene. Her door flung open and out she came fuming, heading towards her mom's door. She grabbed the doorknob but couldn't turn the handle.

Let me get a butter knife to pop the lock.

After getting a knife, she returned to the door and jimmied the lock till the door opened.

"Hang it up! Hang up the. ….."

Some Memories are burned in the mind, like your first love, your prom, your wedding, and the birth of your first born, or in Jolene's case, complaining the phone being hung up and seeing her mom spinning with the ceiling fan.

The note read:

"I'm sorry for the choice I've made,
I had to leave. I'm an empty space
in this home and earth. No love will
be lost, because no one loved me,
even though I loved everyone, not
even the one I gave life to, she
sucked the life out of me and made
me realize that the road I've
traveled was a dead-end. Love you,
And Good Bye."

Jolene had great remorse as the cops
and ambulances left and child
protection just showed. Jolene
didn't know how good she had it.
Had to move in with a distant uncle
in Minnesota. Naturally gripped,

wanting to live with Jack. But it was living with her uncle or a foster home, and she wasn't having that, so she went to the uncle.

It was a hectic night at Saint Joseph's Hospital, shootings, babies being delivered, etcetera. Nate had to be assertive to reach the triage desk then to see his mom.

"Whew, it's a busy night here, huh?" Nate said.

"Just one moment sir," said the receptionist.

"Ok, I'll just find a seat..." Nate looked around the room. It was packed, so he stood against the wall.

Someone was yelling, as the paramedic strolled them in, "Those damn Thugs shot me. You can't even live life without those ignorant hoodlums trying to take it. What's wrong with the people today?"
The person with the shooting victim said,
"People have lost their way and their minds."

After ten minutes, the doctors approached him. "Hello, Nate. Could you come with us? "Ok," Nate replied.

Every nerve in his body was on edge, and his heart was beating so hard through his throat he heard his pulse. He gulped when they got to his mother's room.

One of the doctors turned to Nate and said, "At 6:03 PM your mom, Elizabeth Jane Smith, passed in her sleep. Nate dropped to his knees and burst into tears

Nate got right up and ran to his mother's side and hugged her and said, "I didn't mean to leave you. I'm so sorry mom. I didn't mean to" the medics started to tear up.

Beep, Beep…. Beep, Beep Paul

reached for his cell, as he was putting up his cart. There was a text from Nate.

"Can you come and get me from Saint Joes? This is Nate."

Paul texted back, "Is everything Ok? Nate   "I'll explain everything to you if you can come and get me."

Paul texted back, Yes, I'll come and get you in ten minutes."

Return text from Nate, "Thanks."

"No problem" sent from Paul.

Nate walked outside and sat on a bench and sulked. Every feeling he had in his body was numb as if he took a bath in Novocain.

"Excuse me, sir, did you lose
someone?" a passerby stopped to
ask.

"Why you ask?" said Nate.

You just have the look of lost"

I lost my best friend, my mom."

"I'm so sorry for your loss," said
the concerned lady.

"Thanks," said Nate. Then she left.

Nate slumped as his chin sank
further into his chest, as he awaited
a ride.

After dozing off for five minutes,
Nate was awakened by Paul's horn.

"Hey Nate," said Paul.

"Hey, thanks for picking me up,"
said Nate as he got in.

"It was my mom," said Nate. I lost my mom today. I left her Alone because Jolene was a total bitch. Sorry, she's a mean heartless, and always will be.

"Why you say that Nate?" Paul inquired.

"Because I asked, no I begged, her to take today off," Nate explained. "She said 'no.' You know the thing that moral support can sometimes pull a person through to wellness by knowing someone they love is there for them and the power of touch and prayer? Sorry, my words are jumbled, but you get what I'm saying.   Should have been there damn it. I'm a shitty son

"No, you're not, Nate. We work for shitty people, and for shitty wages," said Paul. *"Don't beat yourself up. You're a nice, caring person and you will be ok in the long run."*

"I know, Paul. I know. Ah thanks again for lifting my spirits and picking me up and taking me home," said Nate.

"No problem, buddy," said Paul. *"So how was your day, Paul?" asked Nate. "It was a good day for a change,"* Paul replied. *"I met a nice girl who I dig."*

"Oh.......... aren't you married to Stacey? Nate responded. *Legally*

Yeah, but she left me last week for some dude she met online, but I'm not going to sit up and mope about it. I got to live and I shall," said Paul.

"Cool you deserve it, Paul," Nate responded.

"Yeah, thanks, Nate. This is my year to shine and to get people to notice me," said Paul.

"Well, good for you," replied Nate. "Hey, maybe your girl can hook me up with a friend?"

Paul replied, *"Yeah I'll ask her who knows. Here you go, your home."*

"Ok, thanks again, friend. See you Monday," said Nate.

"Ok see you, and be strong man,"

said Paul. "I'll try," Nate

Replied and got out of the car and walked to his building.

Paul got home minutes later and jumped in the shower just in case Amber came through for a nightcap. *"Whew, I'm musty." I forgot to put on deodorant earlier because I was running late* though, said Paul to himself.

Halfway through his shower, he got a text message. He quickly got out and fell on his ass, thinking the obvious.

Embarrassed and got up and looked

at his phone, but it was from an unidentified number 000-000-0000 and the text read, "WHO IS THIS?"

Paul stood there puzzled and wet. He put the phone back and continued with his shower, wondering, and quested himself, *"Was I careful? Being sloppy with my crimes? "Be Calm, Ole Pauli. You did well. You covered your tracks.*

Ok, whew, you shouldn't get jumpy at the unknown."

His phone alerted again. Then a chill went up to his spine. He shrugged it off and kept continuing cleansing.

Beep Beep. Paul dropped the soap then he bent over and grabbed it. Beep Beep. Went from being scared to anger off with the constant messages.

Paul finished his shower and dried off then got dressed in his PJ's and then sat on his couch to read all his texts, *"Wishing that all of them was from Amber."*

"Oh shit! I forgot to put on deodorant again", thought Paul. He threw his phone on the couch, and he went to the bathroom to put it on,

as the Oddball, he counts the number of strokes under each armpit, ten for each.

"Now I'm protected," said Paul and back to the couch he came. "Let me see if my baby texted me, '13 texts.'

"WHO IS THIS" skip I read that one.

"Hey answer me back!!"

"Hello!!"

"Hello!!"

"Hey, My brother had this number as his last text,"

"Maybe you know what happened to him?"

No text from Amber, just one from someone else.

"I guess I did slip up. I should have changed my cell number. Shit!!! Let me think. Shit!! Um, I got it," thought Paul.

Paul picked up the phone and texted back, "Hello I'm sorry." Was in the shower. Just got this number two days ago and I've been getting a lot of wrong texts and calls since I got this new phone.   Figured it's something that everyone goes through Send.

"Whew, damn you're smart," said Paul to himself.

Beep Beep. "Hi, I'm so sorry. My name is Jane. My brother went missing about two weeks ago. I don't want to be a bother but can I call you? I just need someone to talk to."

"Sure, you can call me, By the way, I'm Paul. Give me five minutes," replied Paul

"Ok," Jane messaged

Paul went to the kitchen to get himself a quick bite to eat. Two minutes later Paul came out of the kitchen with a plate of pizza bites and a can of soda. He scarfed it within minutes.

Ring. *"It's Jane. Shit! I don't know her* thought Paul before he answered.

"Hello, " Paul speaking.

"Hey, it's Jane."

"Hi, Jane. How are you? "

"I'm ok and you Paul?"

"I'm good now, " Paul replied.

"Why is that?" asked Jane.

"Well, I don't talk to females that much since my wife left me two months ago with her lover, " confided Paul.

"I'm so sorry," said Jane.

"Thanks, but it's ok, " said Paul.

"So, tell me about yourself, Jane, " asked Paul.

'I'm single, thirty and I work for the D.M.V. I have a two-bedroom apartment and two lovely cats. I think I'm cute, but somehow I'm invisible to the world of men," Jane shared. "Maybe it's because I don't show-off my goodies to everyone like some women do these days. *I understand you have to leave something to the imagination."*

Paul Said and laughed then Jane followed with a giggle.

"Thanks, " said Paul. *"That was a good one." It seems like I met you before. I feel so comfortable just this quick, "* said Paul.

"Oh really? Thanks, just don't

break out with the 'You're my soul mate' crud that some people spew out. I mean that if someone clicks with someone, it's just called compatibility and that's it.   Said Jane "OK," said Paul. "I felt neither way about my wife."

"So why'd you get married?" said Jane.

"I don't know. I'll have to get back to you on that one," Paul replied. Jane laughed then Paul laughed.

"Would you like to go out and get some coffee, Paul, one day?" asked Jane.

"Oh yeah, how about now? I know this coffee shop that's open 24 hours. Huh I guess the customers

can't sleep, so they cater day and night, For the Java Freaks," said Paul.

"Yep sure, give me the address, and I'll be there in about thirty minutes. Never mind. I can Search it and what will you be wearing, asked Jane. *"Well, now my Pajamas,"* said, Paul.

"Oh kinky and I'll be wearing a bra and panties," said Jane. *"Hot,"* said Paul. *"I'll be looking for those."*

"Not until we're married!" said Jane. Then they both laughed.

"I'll be in a yellow blouse and black pants to shrink my fat ass." said Jane.

"Oh, I like fat asses," said Paul.

"I bet you do," said Jane, "and you?"

"I'll be wearing a punk-rock t-shirt and jeans with glasses," said Paul.

"Oh, how original and what group would that be?" inquired Jane.

"The Ramones," said Paul.

"I like them," said Jane, plus the X-ray-spex and the Distillers and the Slits."

"Oh, I like Slits," said Paul.

"I bet you do," said Jane.

"So, you like hairy or shaved slits, Mr. Paul?" asked Jane.

"Any, as long as it's clean, I'm in between," Paul replied.

They laughed, and Jane said, "On that note, let me get ready Freddie."

"Ok, me too. So I'll see you there," said Paul.

"Ok see you, Hun," Jane replied.

Then they both hung up

"Man oh man she strikes a nerve in me, wow," thought Paul.

"Damn he could be the one I don't know why, but I have a good feeling about this one," said Jane to herself.

So, they both got ready to meet at The Java Freaks Coffee Shop.

Paul was very punctual and arrived there first, so he got a chance to pick the seating. He chose a cozy booth in the back corner next to the window. And checked his watch as he's always done, his habits. This can be taken the wrong way in some cases during sex, but the only way he could pull it off is in the doggy or reverse cowgirl position. He opened one of the two menus placed on the table by the waitress. *"That looks good. I should order it, thinking all I had was pizza bites for dinner."*

"Hello, may I take your order?"
"Um, someone is joining me, and it would be rude, to order before they get here, especially when I'm trying to make a good impression," said Paul.
"IMPRESSION? Huh? For Me?"

Paul heard a stern voice out the blue from behind the waitress, and his eyes got as big as a pizza pie and got a frog stuck in his throat like an alligator. *"Ah um,"* a short fiery blonde stepped out from behind and said "Paul?"

Chapter 12:

Love and Murder is in the Air.

"Hello, I'm here to see the doctor," said the young woman standing at the counter.

"Ok, one moment please," said the receptionist.

Minutes later she returned "Sorry for the delay, Miss. What seems to be the problem?"

"I'm having trouble sleeping, and my breathing is off," Miss Franks replied.

"Well, due to the severity of your situation I'll fit you in today, it's has been a packed house".

"Ok thanks," said Fran Franks.

The receptionist typed in the
appointment and turned to the
young lady in front of her and said,
"What's your doctor's name?"

"Bill," the woman replied.

"Ok have a seat, and I'll let him
know that you're here," said the
receptionist.

"Thanks." As the young lady took a
seat and sighed with a worried look
on her face as she saw patients in
the room, including the crying
babies, a man in pain, and a teen
that have secrets of a sexual
indiscretion gone wrong, and
wondering why it burns and itches

wishing abstinence was his virtue. Her stomach sank, and her esophagus shrunk then she got up and ran to the lady's room. After she finished her confessions to the porcelain god, she left the restroom, they called her name.

As the phone rang, George was in the shower, so he didn't hear it. He shouted in happiness, "It's Saturday! It's Saturday! It's Mother Fucking Saturday!!! Yeah!" Then George fell quiet because of a strange feeling. "I think someone called me," he thought to himself. "I'm not psychic, but I know." George hurried out of the shower

and ran to his cell phone with a
towel wrapped around him. He got
one missed call from Rosa

Ring Ring….   Ring…." Leave a
message after the beep."
    BEEP………. "Hi honey, is
    everything's ok? Um, call
    me back when you can.
    Love you. Bye." George
    put his cell phone on the
    dresser and walked to the
    kitchen to make breakfast.
    He first put on a pot of
    coffee, grabbed two eggs,
    cheese, bacon, and bread.

A lot of times George just grabs stuff out of the blue and slaps meals together on the go. After ten minutes George put together his E.C.B and got juice from the fridge and sat. He grabbed his sandwich and raised it to his mouth for the first taste of his creation and opened and…

Ring….Ring.

"Oh shit! It never fails," thought George as he put the food back on the plate.

"Ugh, yeah?" said George as he answered the phone

without noticing the number. "Oh, am I disturbing you?" said Rosa. "No baby. I always have time for you. Hell, I'll get off the phone with my mom for you," said George. "Oh honey, you better not, but, I have something to tell you," Rosa said.

George cleared his throat and said, "Ok, tell me."

"I don't want you to be mad at me or hate me but (after a long pause)...........I'm pregnant!!!" Rosa blurted out.

"I'll be right over," said George.

Mixed feelings filled his heart and tears welled up in his eyes. "Shit, how can I afford to be a father with these wages? I thought I was careful. Damn shit, shit maybe it's not mine. Yeah that's it she cheated on me. Damn, I'm going crazy in such a short time. I got to pull it together. I have to."

George got into his car and headed to Rosa's house.

He had a lump in his throat
the size of a pumpkin and
for once in his life, he was
terrified. Not like the
monster under the bed, 'the
Police knocking on your
door scared"!!

He pulled up in front of her
house and got out of the
car, and walked up the
stairs slowly, held and
released his breath then
knocked on the door. Then
the minute he laid eyes on
his Rosa every doubt and
fear in his heart vanished

and what ran through his thoughts was, "This is a good thing. It's a great thing."

"Wow, I'm glad it's Saturday, and I got to figure out what I'm doing today. It would be nice if I can see Jane again. Oh damn, I forgot all about Amber. Hmm, well I'm hooking up with somebody today!" Thought Paul.

Ever since Stacey was out of his life, Paul gained a

Standard testosterone level, so he had the thirst to engage in kinds of coital behavior. But with Jane, he knew he had to take it slow. Ring ......Ring

"Hello," Paul answered

Silence "How can I help you?" Paul replied louder to the caller.

"Hey, it's Amber,"

"Hi," said Paul.

"Sorry I haven't called you

I've been busy," Amber explained.

"It's ok. I've been busy as well" said Paul.

"So what're you doing now," Amber asked.

"Um, nothing. I was going to get into the shower," Paul replied.

"Wait until I get there. Then we can take one together," suggested Amber.

"I'll wait." Paul agreed.

Paul sat on the couch and exhaled, *"I love this new life, no rules, no drama, and no wife."* As he looked up a grin, Paul thought, *"Yeah, I'm boss of my world. Shouldn't have gotten married, all the fun I've could have had after high school. I could have gone to college and spewed my seed all around the campus and not have learned a damn thing...Is talking to myself sane? Hell, I'm a killer. I checked my sanity at the loony bend resort a while ago,"* Paul said to himself.

On his kitchen counter, he
has his vitamins lined up by
size, an actual trait of an
OCD Virgo. After leaving
the kitchen, with vitamins
in one hand and juice in the
other, Paul sat and took
them one by one, chewing
each, has a fear of choking.

"I'm done. Ugh, so bitter.
My bucket list, learn to
swallow pills.   Let me see
what's on TV." Paul
grabbed the remote and
powered it. Golf – "Nope –
click. Tennis – "Nada –

click. Women's Softball
Tournament – "Hell yeah.
Damn look at the pitcher.
She has a nice ass and not a
bad mug either," Paul
observed. Minutes later *a
hard knock at the door "Oh
shit must have dozed-off
that quickly."*
"HOLD ON," Paul yelled,
as he stumbled to the door.
He looked through the peek
hole and saw the redheaded
siren, "Oh, it's Amber," and
Paul unlocked the door.

"Hey what took so long,"

Amber asked.

"Sorry," Paul replied. *"I fell asleep watching the sports and stuff. Come in. Sorry, I have to take a leak. Make yourself at home."*

"Ok. Hey, I'll hold it for you?" Amber teased.

"No, I can manage, but thanks though," said Paul.

"Geeze, *I got to have privacy. What's next? She wants to wipe my ass? Yuck!"* Paul thought and smiled to himself.

As he was relieving himself, he shouted, *"Do you want me to start the water?"*

"You didn't have to yell. I was by the bathroom," said Amber.

"Oh you startled me," Paul said while flushing the toilet.

"Sorry. I was just waiting for you to get out so I can get a kiss and hug. I missed you, Paul," said Amber

"Oh, ok, thanks. I'm cutting the water on," Paul replied.

Amber looked puzzled as Paul shrugged her off. They both got in the shower Paul was in the front as Amber stood shivering in the back. So what's new?

"Nothing much besides working, cleaning my house and yeah I've been busy killing people," Paul replied.

Amber burst out laughing.

Paul stood tight-lipped then Amber gave him a seductive hug and started kissing him on the neck.

Paul closed his eyes in awe.
Amber reached around to
Paul's penis and began
stroking and whispered in
his ear, "I missed you." She
knew a different reaction
would be given after she
seduces him.

"I missed you too," uttered
Paul.

They went at it like two
dogs caught in the rain,
their hearts beating loud as
the thunder, as the wind
was their breath and the

passion was the storm that
surrounded them. After
they dried off, they retired
to the bedroom for a nap.
"Damn that was good,"
said Paul
"Yes," replied Amber Then
silence fell between them
and off to sleep they went.

Amber was awakened by
something touching her
foot. "Huh?" but saw
nothing and went back to
sleep. Minutes later, it
occurred again but harder.
She mumbled, "I must be

nuts. I'm feeling things,"
and drifted back.

Not one minute later,
"Boom." Amber pulled off
the bed. "What the fuck!"
she said, face down. Amber
slowly turned over and saw
the silhouette of a woman
at her feet. She laid there
frozen with terror.

He murdered me," she
spoke. "Get Out! Get Out!
Paul murdered me. You're
next!!" Then in a flash, she
was gone.

Amber just laid there trying to piece together what had just happened.

Then she thought about what Paul said earlier 'I killed people' and jumped up and ran to the living room to get her clothes. Good thing Amber had a one piece and sandals. She unlocked the door and ran to her car, tugged on the door.

"Oh shit, my car keys are in my purse. FUCK!"

Amber Dreaded going back

into the house.

She stood there and contemplating. "How can you be so fucking dumb?" But even as she downed herself, she knew she had to return. So, she put one foot in front of the other like a death row inmate on his steps to his execution. Up the stairs, she went and crept back in. Amber peeked into the bedroom to see if Paul was still sleeping. "Yes!!! He is. Now, where is my damn purse?"

Amber turned around and
saw it was on the couch,
"Cool" I'll be glad to get
the fuck out of here,"
extended her arm to grab
her purse. She felt a
burning pain in her back.
"Ouch, what the fuck," as
she looked down and saw
something silver and red
pierce through her chest,
then everything became
fuzzy, then black.

A trick Paul learned from
Stacey was how to make it
look like you're still in bed.

Paul figured out he had to get Amber to the kitchen quick and in a bag so he could drag her to the basement without making a big mess.

Amber was shaking and quelling so he got the meat tenderizer and whacked her in the head to knock her out. Paul got two black bags, opened them and slid Amber in it feet first.

Beep Beep.
"OH, not fucking now!

Shit. They got to wait. Shit!" stressed Paul and focused on the job at hand.

He doubled then twist tied it. *"Whoa, wasn't that heavy when she was riding me. Amber must have packed on the pounds since I last seen her. Must have been all the fast food,"* it *will kill you* said, Paul, as he dragged her to the freezer.

"Oh, let me check my text message," thought Paul.

"Hey, Paul. This is Jane. I'm in the neighborhood. I could be there in five. Hit me back."

"Damn that was five minutes ago. Shit" panicked Paul.

He replied to Jane, "Hey give me ten minutes in the shower, and I'll let you in."

"Let me hurry this up," thought Paul. He threw in jabs with his knife to make sure she was dead then tossed her in the freezer. Paul headed back upstairs

for a quick look around and clean. He noticed small streaks of blood on the kitchen floor.

"That doesn't even need a mop." A few towels, orange cleaner and it was done. Paul dabbed it up and washed his hands and rinsed the knife.

Ding Dong.

Paul ran to the living room and yelled, "Hold on one second."

"Shit," he noticed more blood on the rug and ran to

the kitchen for more paper towels and cleanser. Paul cut his finger on purpose and rapped it up for a cover-up, in case questions popped up because Paul couldn't do a thorough cleanup job in one minute. Paul chopped an apple and sat it on the coffee table to explain the reason for the cut, dabbed up the blood and flushed the paper in seconds flat.

"Whew," said Paul, as he ran to the door then opened

it. *"Hey, Jane, nice to see you,"*

"Hey Paul," Jane replied.

"Come on in," said Paul.

"I tried to park out front, but somebody parked right in front of your house," said Jane.

"Yeah, the neighbors are rude," explained Paul.

Then, out of the corner of his eye, he noticed Amber's purse, which was the same color as the couch. *"Oh, let me get your jacket, and I'll give you a small tour of my home,"* said Paul.

He carried Jane's jacket in his right hand and scooped up the purse with his left, unnoticed by Jane.

Paul hung up her belongings and threw Amber's bag in the back of the closet.

"Damn that was close," Paul thought.

"What happened to your hand?" asked Jane.

"I cut my finger slicing an apple after I got out of the shower. I'm so clumsy," Paul explained.

"We're all clumsy, but I'm

here, I can cook and cut for you," said Jane with a girlish glee on her face.

"Oh, thanks. I need to be taken care of, and I'll do the same for you said, Paul.

"Aww, isn't that sweet," Jane said, as she extended her arms to hug Paul.

Paul leaned forward to receive a hug but kept his wounded hand at a distance.

"What kind of hug was that?" Asked Jane.

"Huh?" Paul questioned.

Jane replied. That's the kind of hug you give a grandmother or an aunt with halitosis. "Give me love Boy."

"Hey, I'm trying to keep blood off you, Miss."

"Don't worry. I'm not a prissy posh queen," said Jane as she tackled Paul to the floor

They kissed ever so passionately as their hands ran free over their bodies. Paul caressed her breasts feeling her erect nipples

through her sports bra then
traveled to her inner thighs
and in between her legs –
jackpot, as she moaned
yearning for more.

His hands weren't the only
busy ones. Jane hands
rubbed his back and
traveled to his ass and then
to his erect penis. "Damn
you're hard as hell, and I
want you now Paul," Jane
whispered in his ear.
"I want you too," said
Paul.
"Wait. Do you have

condoms?" asked Jane.

"Oh yeah, I do," said Paul when he got up with a boner protruding through his shorts. As he dug into the dresser drawer. Jane stripped behind his back, then she grabbed him around his waist before he found one.

"Damn it's been a long time. You must be very special," said Jane.

"I found them," said Paul, and turned around and saw a naked Jane standing there before him.

She jumped on the bed and
said, "Come hither, mister."
Paul blushed and submitted
to Jane's call and climbed
into bed and made love.

Paul gave each part of
Jane's body even amounts
of attention.
"Oh Paul, I'm yours, yours
for the taking, then a pause
…. For life," said
Jane as she dug her nails
deep in his back, as he
plowed deep in her.
"Ouch, "Said Paul

"I'm sorry," said Jane.

"No problem. Scratch my
back up baby," said Paul as
he started again.

After they were done, Jane
got dressed and said, "I
have to go work Sweetie.

"No problem," said Paul,
then gave her a deep kiss.

"I needed that." *"You're
welcome,"* said Paul.

They walked to the front
door, and then a thud

sounded from the basement, "What's that," said Jane.

"That's my water heater. It randomly makes noises that scare me in middle of the night. It sometimes sounds like a ghost, but I know it's that damn tank," said Paul.

"Oh ok," you should get that checked out, in fact, I know a guy that owes me a favor said, Jane.

Paul shook his head and said *ok* as she hugged Paul then slapped him on the ass. They both giggled while he unlocked the door.

"Ok see you," said Jane.

"See you," said Paul as he closed the door and waited until she pulled off, then he headed slowly to the basement door. *What the fuck was that noise!!* He cut on the lights and headed down the stairs and then there was Amber halfway out of the bag rolling around and knocking stuff over.

"I'm such a lazy killer, "said Paul. They *should call me a slacker whacker,*

not in a masturbatory sense, because no matter how tired a man is, he has enough strength to jerk-off," thought Paul.

"What to do." Sometimes the solution is in front of you, oh, suffocation." Paul grabbed a small plastic bag and put it over Amber's head and closed it tight around her neck and as her life was ending with tears in her eyes, regretting arguing with her parents, running away from home,

her lifestyle, her job and leaving her purse.

Paul left his victim in the basement and went upstairs to check his phone - 2 missed calls (Jane) and two text messages.

"Hey, where are you mister?" Jane's 1st.
"You got what you wanted, and you can't give a sister a response LOL just kidding hit me back when you can sweetie ☺XOXO" Jane's 2nd.

Paul changed into his pajamas and got in bed. Then Paul responded to Jane. "Hey, I left my phone at home when I went to the store I just got back, but I'm here for you now - Send.

He got up and cut the lights off and laid there until he either got a call or a text. Then Paul dozed off.

Beep Beep, *"Huh, who's this?"* Paul wondered.

Paul's eyes where so blurry

and he couldn't make out the text at first, then he focusses on the words that read, "I can't breathe, I can't breathe, why can't I breathe, why?"

Paul was so shaken that he ran to the kitchen to grab a knife and locked his bedroom door then sat on the floor at the foot of the bed with his back to the wall. He didn't even want his cell phone near him, not knowing what other messages would come his way, ignoring all through the night until dawn broke, the light was his safety.

Confused and tired as He stood up and unlocked the door.
He scoped out the sound space of his home with his sonic ears" His paranoia didn't help either. *"Man, I got to stop killing in my home! "Damn, I didn't sleep a wink last night it's becoming a drag and messing with my nerves* said, Paul.

Paul loves hot water when he bathes or showers, as a child, he wasn't allowed to use the hot water not even in the wintertime. "Paul doesn't run the hot water because it will run up my heating bill," his father rammed down his throat. Cold baths were unbearable, but his hatred for his family kept him warm.

Paul started showering. *"What the hell!"* for air out

the blue, he had a panic attack. He got out the shower holding his chest, panting like a dog on a hot summer day. *"What the fuck?* Whew," said Paul, as whatever that had happened ended. He cleared the mirror with his hand so he could see. Suddenly, he saw a shadowy figure leave the bathroom.

"Must be losing it, I'm seeing things. It must be stress. "Yes, its stress what else it could be? But why am I stressed?* "Paul Said

to himself as he dried off and put on his clothes, and threw his dirty clothes in the hamper. *"Damn it's full. Kind of scared to go into the basement right now,"* Paul thought to himself with fear in his heart. *"Need to stop shitting where I sleep, need to have a strategy. Must dispose of Amber and get some sage to rid my home of the bad Omens because that could put a damper on my social life.* After getting dressed, Paul took a big gulp as he headed into the basement with a knife and a bag of laundry not knowing what to expect. *"Chicken shit"* he called himself as he crept down the stairs. *"WTF, I'm a killer,"* he boasted, then jumped as he heard a banging noise, but this time it was the water heater.

Paul looked around, and everything seemed in place, besides the trash bag in the middle of the floor with a body inside of it. He walked up to the deep freezer, reached behind it, got the cord and plugged it in. *"I can put her in the freezer till Tuesday. With her being frozen, it'll be easier to break her up to get rid of her for good this time Paul planned."*

Chapter 13:
A Start, To a Mean.

Nathan heals in his apartment, warm beer in one hand, a photo album in the other and in his lap lays bunches of used tissues, stagnant unshaved and unbathed since the passing of his mother.

Nate called his friend.

Ring...... Ring.

"Hello"

"Hey Paul, this is Nate then a pause....... Sorry to disturb you. I just needed to talk to someone," said Nate.

"Agh," coming from Paul's end of the line.

Then Nate heard a crash. "Is everything Ok?"

After silence *"Hey Nate just throwing out the trash and I dropped my phone in the process, sorry,"* said Paul.

"Um, I can call back later if you're busy," said Nate.

"No, I'm good," said Paul.

"So, what's up, Nate?".

Needed someone to talk to and I know I sound like A broken record said, Nate. "I've been in a real funk and needed something different."

"Hey, why don't we have a boy's night out, since we don't have to work Monday because of the holiday, Paul suggested.

"Hey, that sounds good. That's why I knew to call you," said Nate.

"Hey, you can't just sit home and rot. And besides, what would your mom say? I want you to live your life to the fullest" said Paul, Nate cracked the biggest smile in years as if she was speaking through him like a message sent from *heaven "I must do a couple things, and I'll pick you up about six, and it's on me! My treat."*

"Oh, thanks. You're a lifesaver," said Nate.

With a smirk, *"Sure, I guess, I am."*
"Ok See you then," said Nate.
"Ok... Bye."

"I guess, let me get up and get shaven and showered. Whew, is that me or does a horse live here with that smell, whew?" observed Nate.

Nate collected the tissues, beer cans that surrounded him on the sofa and floor into a trash bag. "Before I get into the shower, I must spray the couch, because I know my smell is mugging up the place," thought Nate.
Nate cleaned the kitchen, the bathroom, vacuumed the

Livingroom and took out the trash before he got into the shower.

Ring……. Ring.

"Hello," Paul answered.

"Hey what are you doing?" asked Jane.

"Nothing now but I have plans after six o'clock."

"And that would be?"   she inquired.

"If you must know…," Paul began in reply.

Jane interrupted, "I do."

"I'm having a boys' night out for my friend who just lost his mom. He needs to get out of the house," explained Paul.

"Awe, what a great friend to think

of him, in time of need,"

said Jane. "Thanks," said Paul.

Hey, can I shoot on by for a

quickie?

"Sure, but it wouldn't have to be

that quick. I still have three hours

till I leave," said Paul.

"Ok, I'll be on my way," said Jane.

"Ok

Sweetie"

"Oh damn! I still must call George

to see about his plans for tonight

said, Paul. Ring…. Ring "Hello,"

answered George.

"Is this George?" inquired Paul.

"Yeah …. who is this?" said

George.

"Hey, it's Paul. Do you have any

plans tonight?"

Not that I know of, why? *"I'm*
throwing a boys' night out for
Nathan. Are you in?" asked Paul.

"Sounds good let me call my girl to
double check," said George, OK
talk to you then," replied Paul.

"I need to install a latch on the
freezer then put a lock on it, in case
I have some company tonight after
the bar. *Wait a minute, Jane's on the*
way. Shit!! Too many things so little
time Thought Paul.

Ring……….. Ring
"Hello," said Rosa.

"Rosa, hey you don't need me tonight, do you?" asked George.

"No, Why? Where are you going and who are you going with?"

"Um, gasp, just going out with co-workers for beers," Said George.

"Male or Female or both?" she questioned.

"Just guys. It's a boys' night out thingy," said George,

"I see, well you better behave. mister,"

"you have nothing to worry about my love. You are my world," George assured her.

"You're so sweet. I thought I was your city or your block,"

"Ha, you're so funny. Let me get

ready," said George.

"Ok babe," Rosa responded, "bye."

Let me call Paul to confirm for tonight.

Ring…… Ring.

"Hello," Paul answered.

"Hey, I'm in," George said.

"Cool, I'll come and get you at 6:30," said Paul.

"Ok sounds good. I'll text you my address, text me when you're here so I can come right out" said George.

"Ok will do," said Paul.

As the evening came, the guys got dressed, with pressed linens, cologne they sprayed filled the air as testosterone pumped through their veins. Paul grabbed his keys and headed to the car. *"Damn*

I have to get gas".
"$3.90 a gallon. Shit, it was just $3.20 last week. Gees Louise,"
Thank Goodness I have a small car thought Paul

Paul pulled into the gas station. It was crowded for a Sunday. Paul parked in front of a pump and didn't notice the guy behind him honking his horn. Paul got out of his car to walk into the station.

"Hey, Fucker!!!" Paul heard yelled

from behind him but didn't pay it no mind.

"Hi, can I have twenty on pump seven?" Paul asked the attendant.

"Sure," said the attendant as Paul slid the bill on the counter.

"Thanks," said Paul and he walked back out the door.

"Hey little fucker, you cut me off! Said the driver behind.

"Oh sorry, I didn't know," said Paul.

"Hurry and get your gas before I get pissed," the driver threatened.

"Calm down," said his Girlfriend.

"Shut the fuck up Bitch! If I wanted your input, I would have asked. Oh, I never do, so I guess, zip it!" said the angry driver.

"So, I guess another bad boy chew toy. What a shame. She's cute. Paul said under his breath as he waited for the gas to stop flowing. *"Good, finished,"* then Paul hung up the pump and got in his car.

Honk......... Honk. "Bout time! Shit!! I should have kicked his ass I should've," he blurted to his girlfriend, as he pulled up to the pump while Paul pulled out...

"Let me pick up Nate first since he's closer," planned Paul.
After he pulled in front of Nate's place Paul texted him, "I'm out

front."

"Paul sat there contemplating on where they are going, and in what order.

Fuck it lets wing it, but that's out of order, of my structured mind frame. Damn, I'm shocked I didn't plan way ahead. Wow, you are so fucking dumb and stupid Paul," he whispered to himself.

After the abuse by his family, Paul internalized self-criticism, the verbal the aspect of his abuse. Everything he does is not good enough, not even for himself.

Beep…. Beep.

"Give me five minutes, and I'll be right out," texted Nate.

"Ok," Paul replied. Then he reached into his glove compartment and pulled out his notepad and wrote down ideas of places to go and things to do.

Knock Knock.

"Hey, Paul," said Nate. Paul snapped out of his train of thought with pen in hand and an empty front sheet on his notepad. As he opened the door and Nate got in, Paul still had a puzzled expression on his face as if he woke up from a cat nap.

"Hey what were you writing?" Nate asked.

"Nothing," said Paul. *"I was thinking of making a spreadsheet of our activities."*

Nate suggested, "We should just go with the flow, but start off with some food, I'm starving," Nate said.

"Hey, that's sounds good. I'll follow your lead!!" said Paul as he pulled out from his parking spot. *"Hey, can you call George and let him know we're on our way? Here's my phone. I'm not a big talk and text person when behind the wheel. I'm not trying to hurt or kill people. It's all about safety,"* with a grin said, Paul.

Ring…Ring.

"Hello," George answered the phone.

"George its Nate. I'm calling from Paul's phone. What's your address, because we're on our way?" said Nate. "1422 Wall St," George responded.

"Ok, I know where you are. Give us Five minutes," said Nate.

"Ok, see you then," George replied.

"Ok, said Nate,"

"Hey, Paul I figured we should go to Finnegan's for dinner. They have a buy one, get one half off on meals, and the soft drinks are free," suggested Nate.

"Shit that sounds good," said Paul, "but who gets the fourth meal? I guess we can divide it up 3 ways said, Nate.

"We'll see when we get there," Paul replied as he pulled in front of George's building.

"What up?" said George as he approached the car.

then got in."

"You don't have a curfew, do you?" joked Paul.

"Hell no! George replied. *Cool. I had to ask since you're the only one on lockdown!"* Paul explained.

"I'm in a relationship, but I'm not

married," said George

"NOT YET," barked Nate.

Laughter roared through the car, setting up the mood for the night.

"Woo Hoo. It's a good feeling when just us guys get to hang out. We should have done this before," said Nate

"Damn, pipe down Girls. We haven't even got to the restaurant yet," rebutted Paul with a smile.

George shouted, "We have to go to the strip club. I want to see some tits and ass.

"I second that and third that motion," Paul and Nate agreed.

"But first let's get something to eat," Paul directed.

Minutes later, they pulled in Finnegan's lot and smelled the food from the car. Their stomachs rumbled as the aroma carried them into the place like magic.

"Hello, welcome to Finnegan's. How many in your party?" asked the hostess?

"Just us, three Miss," Paul replied

"Ok, come this way. Do you guys want a booth or a table?" she asked.

A

table please for easier access to the restroom said, Paul.

"Let me get your menus," said the hostess.

"Remember that special I mentioned earlier?" Nate asked.

"I didn't forget," Paul replied. Then suddenly, the restaurant tilted and got smaller to Paul then he got nervous and anxious as his anxiety set in as more people poured in the restaurant. He heard his heartbeat in his ears, and the waitress hadn't even taken their order yet. *"Maybe I should have my order to go,"* thought Paul, *"but what would everyone think? What would they say, that I'm a freak? I don't want to be called a freak. I must be normal, got to be normal, for tonight at least,* thought Paul trying to calm himself. *Why is everyone looking at*

me? I can hear my pulse Along with the Chatter from the other Diners. Let me get up and go to the bathroom," thought Paul

"I'll be right back guys," Paul said to George and Nate. Paul got up to find the restroom but the restaurant was so congested he had to say, *"excuse me"* at least ten before he found it.

Once in, he looked in the mirror and saw his face and realized how flushed he looked. *"What's wrong with you? Get a grip, Come on, Shit! This supposed to be a fun night and you're ruining it fucker. Get rid of your pride and fears."*

Paul said to himself when he cut the
water to wash his hands and face of
the sweat and frustration.

Boom! Paul jumped, *"Oh, I didn't
know there was anyone in here,"* he
whispered to himself as he reached
for a hand towel.

Boom! Paul jumped again and said,
"Are you ok in there?" Then he
heard laughter, but the laughter
sounded like a female. He spoke
with vigor, *"I think you're in the
wrong bathroom."*

Then the laughter stopped, and the
voice said, "You're in the wrong
bathroom."

Huh? This is the men's restroom."

said Paul

The voice replied, "Yes, but you're no man! You're no man. You're no man." Then the voice got faster and louder, "You're no man. You're no man." Then a second voice accompanied the first one, "You're a killer. You're a killer. You're a killer. You're no man. You're a killer. You're no man. You're a killer." Then it all stopped. Paul dashed from the bathroom confused, *"What the hell, he said"* He got back to his seat, *"What did I miss?"*

Nate replied, "Nothing much, But the waitresses and the bartender are hot."

George added, "We know what we want. We were just waiting for you before we order."

"guys, you're so considerate," said Paul. As He Scanned the Menu and decided for himself burger and fries and said, *"We should pick tenders as our fourth meal so we can split them up easy."*

"Ok," from the guys.

"Hi, are you guys ready to order?" asked the waitress. Yes

One after another they told the waitress what they wanted. Then a moment of silence fell upon the group, then a yawn and a sigh.

"Damn look at the group of girls

behind us," Whispered George.

The rest of the guys followed suit glancing at them and. If the waitress had brought their food, they wouldn't have noticed.   Paul, the most observant of the bunch, was scoping out every girl in the place.
Then he saw that one girl at the bar was slouched down with her head in her hands, while everyone else at the bar was very social. Paul was wondering, "Did she have too much to drink or did she get some bad news? Paul was really concerned about her.

Then the waitress showed up with

beverages.   "Here

you go. Your meals should be out

soon."

"Thanks," they responded.

Then Paul looked back at the girl,

and she was gone.

Paul turned back around to have a sip of his soda.
"Where are we going next after this?" asked Paul, "Strip Club?"
"Yeah, the Strip Joint," Nate replied.
"Well that's the plan," said Paul with a sigh.

Within his heart, he was concerned about the girl at the bar.   Then the food arrived
  "about time." *This smell's and looks so good said Paul,* the guys started digging into their meals as if they were Hungry Zombies.

While Paul was eating, he was drawn to one of the TVs on the wall. As a breaking news report Interrupted the Ballgame. "Missing female." Then he saw a picture of Amber on the TV next to the newscaster. Then it cut to an interview of her mother grieving saying why? A chill ran up Paul's spine, and he got nervous.

"What's wrong Paul? You look as if you just seen a ghost, do you know her?" asked George.

"Oh no, I get moved when I see parents in tears over their loss of a loved one," explained Paul.

George turned to the TV, "Oh yeah I

heard of that story. She's missing, not dead yet."

Nate added, "Nine out of ten, she is dead."

"That's what I was saying and thinking," said Paul.

"Well I have a different way of thinking," said George.

I'm optimistic. That's what's wrong with society today. No one believes or has faith anymore.

"Awe George, you want a hug?" teased Paul.

"Hell no!" said George.

"You see. You're losing faith already," Paul said with a smirk.

"No Sir, I am not!" replied George.

"Ok let's divide up these tenders and fries so we can get out of here," Paul stated. Then as he dug into his portion of food, then he felt someone breathing down his neck, but he refused to turn around, after his episode in the bathroom. Paul kept ignoring the distraction and then it stopped. He took a deep breath to relax then he slowly turned around, and no one was there, but the strange girl was back at the bar

"Hey, do you see someone you like Paul?" asked Nate?

"Ah, just worried about that girl at

the bar," Paul replied.

"What girl? All I see over there is dudes. No wonder why you wanted a hug," said George.

"Fuck you," said Paul.

"Thanks', but you're not my type" George replied.

Then laughter broke out at their table, but it was silent by one, as soon as the breathing started again behind Paul's neck.

"Shit! Nobody sees her but me. Am I going crazy? We got to keep it together at least for tonight," to himself Paul thought.

As the fun and laughter carried on

Paul's inner demons were tormenting him. *"Why me?"* he asked himself. Then he thought, *I'm a killer.*

"I need a real drink," Paul said out loud. Then to himself, he said, *"To kill these phantoms in my head."*

"Oh waitress, I need a mudslide," Paul ordered.

The guys laughed at him, "Oh yeah, a real drink."

"Hey, I'm driving, and I can't drink too hard. I could kill someone," Paul laughed.

"Drinking and driving is not a laughing matter dude," Said Nate.

"right, but a mudslide is still a Girly

drink," said George.

"When it comes, you can't get none," replied Paul. "You have to order it first, and by the shitty service from our slow ass waitress Said, Nate. Fuck the drink! I want the check," said Paul. "Let's walk to the counter to pay the cashier.

"I want to pay the bill for that table, and the waitress sucked.
As you can see, she's over there flirting with the hockey players, woohoo who gives a puck," said Paul.

"Oh, I'm so sorry. That waitress is new," said the cashier.

"Whatever," Paul said.

"For your trouble, I'll cut your bill in half," offered the manager who had overheard the conversation.

"Oh thanks," Paul said with a smile.

"no problem," said the manager.

As the guys left a big boom sounded off in the restaurant, but it didn't faze anyone to turn around except Paul, but maybe it was just him who heard it.

They got into the car, and one said, "To the Sugar Shack we go." Then out of the parking lot they left. Beep Beep. *"Damn who texting me? Shit,"* said Paul.

"One of your many many girlfriends," said George.

"Ok funny man.," Paul said, Ok one of your many Boyfriends followed with loud laughter *Good thing you're in the back-seat Paul Noted.* Then They pulled into the Sugar Shack lot, which wasn't far from the restaurant.

Paul checked his Phone *"I never heard of this number."* The text read:

"YOU CAN'T GET AWAY THAT EASY. I WILL FOLLOW YOU, IN THE AFTERLIFE AND FOR ALL ETERNITY."

Paul's face turned flushed again.

"This can't be happening. I got to

show someone this," Paul thought. Then he said out loud, *"Hey look at this text and tell me what you think guys, Ok?"*

Looks like you're getting lucky, said George.

"Huh?" said Paul as he took the phone back. Saw it was a text from Jane. *"Sorry,"* said Paul.

They arrived at the sugar shack, walked through the door

"Hello ID's, and five dollars apiece than a stamp on the back of your hands in case of any smokers, also" No touching or grabbing or Bruce right here will touch and grab you out of here, Said the girl at the door.

"Ok thanks for the heads up," said Paul

"Damn look at that one," "Oh look at this one' as if they were kids in a candy store. So many choices and not enough money. They found a nice seat on the stage were dancers are encased in glass. "Thanks' Paul, for such a fun night," added Nate. Then Paul was Approached by a stripper named Skyler. She whispered in his ear let's have a private lap dance.

She grabbed his hand and pulled him into the V.I.P Room Paul sat in the chair as Skylar started undressing she asked his name, and he answered *its Paul*, then he asked her name, and she replied Skyler. You want to know why I picked you. Because you looked like the Alpha dog of your group, now it's time for me to take charge of you by giving you one hell of a lap dance, you won't soon forget!!

Straddled on top of him she put her arms around him and whispered in his ear I want to fuck you, I want to fuck you hard, Paul nervously replied *Ok I want to fuck you too*. She rode him so hard his dick awakened. Then Skylar stops moving leaned over to his ear and whispered were in this room alone with no cameras. Paul said "*Ok*" she reached and unzipped his fly and pulled out his cock and started stroking. In his ear, Skylar said Oh what a big boy then gripped his cock harder and asked him to do you like it? Paul said *yes oh yes,* she said do you love it? And he replied *hell yeah* Skylar stopped stroking and said isn't it Cold in here? Paul said *what?* Skyler Reply isn't it cold in here? *I don't mind It seems like they have the air conditioner on* replied Paul, she said it's freezing in here, he said *huh?* Then he Notices her voice changed "I can't get out, it's cold in here." I can't get out, I can't get out, and Paul turned his head and notice Skyler's face had ice crystals then Paul yelled and got up then Skylar hit the floor as he ran out of the room and everybody turned their head. Paul ran to the restroom to collect himself.

Man, I'm losing it again.

"Hey, let's get out of here and go to the club," confirmed Paul to the group.

"And it's free to get in this one, except for the drinks, only if you need drinks," said Paul. But what if a nice lady wants a drink we can oblige only if she's hot! Dogs need to find their own way to get tipsy."

"But I digress the homely need love too," Explained Nate.

"Yeah that's called charity," said George followed by big laughs.

Damn, that's mean, said Paul.

As the guys walked in Paul, stated: *"If anyone picks up chicks we can go to my place and crash for the night."*

Then they separated and found their comfort zones: Nate=Pool Table, George=darts, and Paul =the bar.

"What can I get you?" the bartender asked Paul.

"Um let me get a Long Island Ice Tea, " said Paul.

"Coming right up," said the bartender.

As Paul waited for his drink he spun around in his stool to scan the scenery in the bar *"Not even two minutes, and I got one in my scope,"* said Paul to himself.

"Here's your drink said the bartender. *Keep the change,"* said Paul.

"Thanks"

"Where did she go," Paul said to himself. Thinking about the lady as he turned around to enjoy his drink.

"Hey handsome, can I play darts with you?" said a lady who had Stood by George.

"Sure, it's a free country," George

replied.

"That not why I asked you, but luckily, you're cute," said the woman.

"Um, thanks," replied George, as she smacked his ass.

"No problem sweetie," she replied as George smiled and cleared his throat.

"The winner takes all, and I mean all," she said. My name is Suzy."

"Nice to meet you, Suzy. I'm George."

"I love the name George," Suzy said.

"Thanks, can I buy you a drink?" George asked.

"I'm not much of a drinker. I'm

more of a thinker, but thanks for thinking of me," she replied.

"No problem, let's begin our match," said George.

"Are you going to use this table?" the guy asked Nate.

"Nah, I'm just messing about," Nate replied.

"We want to use it for a game," the guy explained.

Ok here you go, would you like to play with us? "Nah I'm not that good," Nate said

"What, your mommy won't let you play?" the guy taunted.

"Well I just lost my mother," said

Nate.

"Oh, Sorry man." I give everybody
shit. That's my nickname, Shit
Giver," the guy explained.

Nate smiled.

"You can just watch the game." said
the guy.

"Ok Mr. Giver," replied Nate.

Laughter broke out.

"You're funny, man. Haha. Ok, let's
rack'em up."

"Excuse me, Sir." Followed by a
light tap on the shoulder. Paul
turned around.

Chapter 14:

The Start of Something

Its 1 am Monday morning, a holiday, and most have the day off, so either people are catching up on rest or still out partying except...

Oh no......., my son's in trouble. Mommy's going to save you."

Dial tone. Beep times seven....Ring... Ring... Ring. "Hi, you've reached George. Sorry I..." click.

Redial. "Hi, you've reached George. Sorry I missed your call. Please leave me a message after the tone, and I'll get back to you as soon as possible." Beep

"Georgy, please call Mommy back, it's an emergency please!!!" Click. "Ah, yeah everybody on the dance floor and shake your ass, shake your mother fuckin ass, Come on!!!" The D.J yelled. So, the people gravitated to the dance floor, even if they

couldn't dance they tried, it
didn't matter everyone was
tipsy.

Paul gave them a nod,
letting them know that
everyone's heading back to
his house because that's
where the real fun starts.
Two o'clock approached
and the guys told their dates
that they're having an
after-party at Paul's home.

Suzy stated, "Anybody
without a ride can come

with me."

George said, "I'll ride with
you,"

"Ok Babe," "Anyone else?"
said Suzy

"Nope. We're going to ride
with Paul, let's get our
belongings, and we can roll
said, George.

As everyone piled into the
cars, it started to rain with a
slight rumble from afar.

The engines began as the
squeak of the wipers joined
the thunder in the
symphony of the night.

On their way to Paul's,
George wanted to check his
cell for any emergencies,
but he didn't out of respect
for Suzy. While she steered
with her left hand, she
grabbed George's hand
caressed his palm.
"Ah, that's smoothing said
George," as he closed his
eyes. But he opened them
thinking of Rosa.

As they parked in front of
Paul's house, the rain
poured harder, so everyone

scurried to get in.

"Oh sorry, my place is such a mess," Paul said.

"It's ok, from one janitor to the next," said Nate.

Paul gave him the stink eye and laughed it off.

"Ok everybody," said Paul. *"let me give you a small tour of my house, The main floor, Here's the bathroom, kitchen and here's the extra bedrooms one with a bed and one without. Don't worry, I got an air mattress you could use."*

"Thanks for everything and

your hospitality Paul," said
Nate.

"No problem," said Paul."
"In the fridge, there's wine
and beer and here are the
cups for you to use. I'm off
to my room. Oh, finally
there was a flood in my
basement, so stay up here if
you don't want to get wet!"
Suzy said, "I don't need to
go into the basement to get
wet." Everyone broke out
in laughter. Paul grabbed
the Air
Mattress and whispered to
his date to go into the

master bedroom. George
pulled a quarter from his
pocket, who going to sleep
on the air mattress,
"You ready Nate?" asked
George.
"Ok I want heads," said
Nate.
"Ok, I'll take tails even
though both are cool
George said with a smirk
and flipped and caught the
coin then slapped it on the
backside of his other hand.
Damn heads you win
Nate."
"Yeah, yes, yes I'm a

winner," said Nate.

"Hey quiet in there, winner," said Paul.

As Paul plugged up the cord and hose to the air compressor, George and Suzy went into the bathroom.

"Oh cool, he has mouthwash," said Suzy as each one of them took a swig and swished it around. The bed was finished filling up. *"Ready Freddy,"* Paul said.

"Ok, I'll meet you in the bedroom George," said

Suzie.

"Ok sweetie," George
replied.

Suzy closed the bathroom
door and sat on the toilet,
"Oh Fuck!" after 30
seconds. "Not now, damn. I
had that feeling as soon as I
left the house, cramps,"
said Suzy to herself. After
the toilet flushed, she crept
out of the bathroom, and
into the room with George.
"Be careful. There are
boxes in here. I learned the
hard way and fell on my

ass," said George sitting in
the chair.

"I have bad news for you,
Honey," began Suzy,

"Let me guess. You got
your period, it's no biggie.
I'll be happy just holding
you," George said
understandingly.

"What are you gay?" Suzy
asked.

"Nope, I'm a gentleman.
We still exist these days.
Don't let the Neanderthals
confuse you," explained

George. Suzy smiled and
hugged him. They both laid
in each other's arms.
Heather asked Nate, do you
have condoms?"
"Oh shit! I'll check and see
if one of the guys has one.
I'll be right back, ok babe.
Nate wrapped himself in
the covers, but he heard
Paul getting busy, so he
didn't knock on that door
and went to the room where
George and Suzy were, and
lightly knocked and said,
"Hey you got a condom?"
"Yeah, here you go," said

George.

"Thanks," as he hurried
back to the room. He
unraveled his sheet and got
in bed and started making
love.

George saw Suzy falling
asleep with her light
snoring in his arms, he
absorbs the sounds of
squeaking beds and moans.
Frustrated with the action
in the house and his film set
closed he shimmied out of
her arms and got up went to
the bathroom, but first, he

put his ear to Nate's door,
"Damn." he whispered, Go
ahead shit. I didn't think
you had it in you." He
smiled as he walked into
the bathroom and closed
the door. Let me check my
phone, "Damn I have ten
missed calls. Damn, I hope
everything's ok.   Three
Messages too."

"Let's see who called me,
hmm eight from mom and
two from Rosa. What the
hell.
"three new voice

messages,"

First message: "Georgie, please call mommy back it's an emergency please!!!"

Click: message save.

New Message: ", I'm scared....... Call mommy back, let me know you're ok please." Click: Message save, again.

New message: "Hey baby this is Rosa. I'm worried. Your mom called me crying and told me you could be in trouble. Call me back baby to let me know you're alright. Love you. Muah."

Click…George pressed save.

No more new messages……Beep. "Let me call Rosa first," George said to himself. Ring ………Ring, "Hey where you at?" asked Rosa. "I'm at Paul's house. I'm ok," said George. "Shit your mom woke me up, and scared the hell out of me, talking crazy," said Rosa. "It's ok, My mom does that sometimes". "When are you coming home?" asked Rosa.

"In the morning," said
George.

"I have a feeling you
should leave now," said
Rosa. "I don't know, your
mom got to me, Shit!"
"It's going to be alright,"
said George.
"Please Baby, promise me,"
begged Rosa.
"I promise," George
assured her.
"Call me when you get in,"
said Rosa.
"Ok, my love, I will,"

"Bye Babe," said Rosa as she reluctantly let him go.

"Ok bye," said George.

"Whew," said George. "I shouldn't even call my mom. I should take my ass straight to bed. Yep, that's what I'm going to do, go nighty night. Let me take a wiz first. Zip, ah damn. It would've been nice to get some though."

Buzz. "Damn." Buzz. "Every time I take a piss somebody's got to call," George said to himself. "Oh no, it's my mom. I'm going to regret this, but oh well."

"Hello," said George.

"Get out of the house now!" his mom instructed.

"What?" asked George, confused?

"Get out of that house!" George's mom emphatically stated.

"Why?" George asked, still not understanding.

"I see blood, old and new blood," said his mom.

"Get out now!! I don't want to bury you. You're supposed to bury me. Listen. Forget the questions."

"Mom are you losing it?"
asked George.

"You don't believe me? My
own son doesn't believe
me.   Well, I'm going
to make you into a
believer," his mom said.
"His name starts with the
letter P." "There's a body in
his freezer. She's the one
that's missing in the news.
His wife and her friend are
gone by his hands. Get your
female friend to drive you
home now!!!"

"What??" George was

having a tough time absorbing what his mom was saying.

"Enough with the questions! Move it, son," George's mom urged.

"Thanks. I will Mom," George answered quietly and left the bathroom and snuck back into the bedroom.

George shook Suzy, and whispered "Hey, hey, hey… we got to go."

"What? Why? I'm so tired," said Suzy.

"Hey, I'll drive you. I have
a license. You can stay at
my place," said George,
trying to convince her.

"Ok, I'll go with you,"
Suzy replied.

"Hey, we have to be very
quiet in leaving here,"
instructed George.

"Seriously?" "Ok, man
you're pushy Suzy said,
But I like that in a
gentleman. Kiss me,
George."

"Ok. Smack. Let's go now,"
urged George.

As they left Paul's home, they Heard him still having sex with his date. "Cool, we're out of there," I promise, I'll explain everything to you, once we get to my place," offered George.

"Ok, I'll wait," Suzy said. George adjusted the mirrors adjusted the driver's seat started the car and drove off. "Whew! Shit! We dodged a bullet," said George.

"Huh?" Suzy said, not understanding what was

going on.

George explained, "My mom, shit she's fucking psychic!"

"Huh, I'm lost," Suzy interjected.

George went on, "The reason we couldn't go in the basement wasn't that of a flood, it was because there's a body in the freezer. My mom saved us. She said it, something was going to go sour tonight.' Damn! I should have gotten Nathan out."

"Maybe nothing's is going

to happen," Suzy reasoned, "Yeah I hope so," said George.

Ten minutes later they arrived at George's apartment building. "Ok, we're here," said George. "How's the security in your building?" asked Suzy. "Airtight. You must ring up for access, and the doors are steel with dead-bolted double locks, and I have a gun. I wish Paul would even think," said George.

"Sounds safe," said Suzy.

"But she – mom - nailed
it," marveled George. "She
mentioned you! She knew
nothing about you! Damn -
Nate....Why? Fuck!"
moaned George filled with
concern for his friend.

"Shush, until we get in.
Then we can talk, ok
babe?" Suzy tried to
comfort George. They got
in George's apartment and
got ready for bed.
"Wait, I'll be right back got
to call my mom," George

said.

"Ok," Suzy replied.

George walked into the living room and sat Down and called.

Ring Ring.

"Hello," George's mom answered.

"Hey, I'm home," George informed her.

"Thanks for listening to me Son. It could have ended horribly,"

"Sorry for your friend you left behind, you could have been killed if you tried to help him," "He thinks very

highly of the P man. mom
explained
"Well, mom his name is
…" George began.
His mom interrupted, "I
don't need to know.
Like the devil, you don't
need to say his name. Did
you call Rosa?"
"Not yet, but I will," said
George.
George's mom interjected,
"Don't! Let me call her.
You have
   a guest, and you shouldn't
be rude. I'm your mother,
keep listening to me, and

you'll be alright. Keep watching the news and keep your eyes and ears open," George's mom cautioned "Ok, I will, love you Mom and thank you for everything," said George. "You too Georgie. Talk to you later," his mom replied. Ok, Bye," said George.

Click.

Beep.

"Ah man," said George as he got up.

"Hey sweetie, I didn't take too long did I," asked

George.

"Nope, I was just laying here thinking," said Suzy.

What…?" said George.

"About you," said Suzy. "I know we just met tonight, but I dig you."

"Hmm I see," said George. "Well, let me tell you what I know, and I dig you too Babe."

Suzy smiled.

"You are an amazing lover. Damn, Paul, you make a girl want to marry you," said Heather.

"Well, I'm not the marrying kind," said Paul. *I tried it once,   but she didn't make the cut, but who can tell what the future holds. I'm going to the kitchen; would you like a water?"* he asked.

"After our workout, I Sure could use a drink," said Heather.

"Ok." *it's quiet out here, I guess everybody fucked themselves to sleep* thought Paul. *"Here you go. One water for the misses,"* said

Paul as he returned to the bedroom.

"Thanks," she said. "Um, I couldn't help but notice you sleep with a knife on your nightstand," she added.

"Yeah, I keep that nearby in case any marauders" explained Paul.

"Oh, cool. I'm tired babe I got to crash I have to babysit tomorrow," she explained.

"I'm a little tired too," said Paul then he rolled over on his stomach.

Paul and his date fell fast asleep. Hours later Paul was awakened by a noise. It sounded as if someone was crying, but Paul was too tired to pay it any mind, so he fell back to sleep. Then he heard a loud scream "Aghhhhh" …Paul woke up and felt the space next to him and notice she was gone.

"Maybe she's in the bathroom," thought Paul, so he laid there for a minute until he heard someone in

the basement.

He shot up, put on his slippers,

and grabbed the knife from the nightstand and quietly went downstairs.

"Hello, I told you to stay out of the basement," said Paul. He cut the light on and saw the freezer door open.

"Hmm, that's funny," to himself he said, as he went to close the door. He heard footsteps creaking up the stairs. Paul turned and said, *"GET BACK HERE YOU*

NOSEY BITCH!!"

She ran up the stairs, before she could scream, Paul caught up with her and covered her mouth with his left hand and stabbed her with his right. She stumbled and fell down the stairs, Boom. Paul kept jabbing 'until she stopped moving.

Then he heard the guest room door open. Then turned and saw Nate's date, rubbing her eyes in the doorway, "Is everything ok down there?" she asked.

"You picked up the wrong guy, and now I have to send you to heaven," said Paul. "Huh?" she asked, confused by his statement. Paul ran up to her wielding his knife like a Samurai. She went down quick. Between the two, they had over 200 knife punctures and lacerations.

Paul peeked into Nate's room. He was still asleep. *"Good,"* Paul whispered. "I'll kill him later, but now

I have to dispose of these two."

One by one, he placed both girls into the freezer. He went back upstairs, got a bucket, a mop, and a sponge and started cleaning from the stairs down to the basement, an hour later he changed from his blood-soaked clothes into overalls.

"Oh shit! I forgot to check on George and his date," thought Paul. *"Well, I'm done in here. Shit, I hate*

cleaning!" Paul mumbled.

Paul froze, as he heard Nate coughing.

"Shit!" said Paul.

Paul first checked George and Suzy room. *"Hmm, nothing. They must have left in the middle of the night. Lucky them,"* thought Paul.

Paul ran to the kitchen to wash off the knife. And tucked it in his back pocket and greeted Nate, *"Hey buddy how did you sleep?"*

"Ah, I slept great. Where is my date?" Nate asked.

"Oh she left and won't be coming back," said Paul.

"Awe damn. I wanted to marry her. She was hot.

"Why did you say she's not coming back?" asked Nate.

"She had an accident and had to leave in a hurry," Paul explained.

"Damn! I just don't get it. Hmm," said Nate.

"In time you will, It will be very crystal to you very soon my friend," said Paul.

"I want to thank you, Paul, for a super time yesterday. I

mean after my mom there was no reason to live," said Nate.

"It's overrated," Paul said.

"Huh? Life is over fucking rated?" asked Nate.

"You live, you die, in between you try, but it's never good enough," said Paul. *"You see I don't fucking care because even as a child my parents treated me like shit. They even got my siblings involved in on the shenanigans, and that shaped me into the man I*

am today," stated Paul. "But you are a great, generous and caring man," said Nate.

"I wish that were true," said Paul, *"but it's not. I'm a killer, pretending to be a janitor to clean up his messes."* Nate laughed, smiled and laid back on the bed.

"Hey, Nate you want to see something cool?" asked Paul. "Sure," Nate replied. *"Follow me. You're going*

to die when you see this," said Paul.

"Sure, buddy," Nate responded.

Paul led Nate into the basement and said, *"I have to tell you the truth. My basement isn't flooded. Sorry for lying to you, but that lie is as good as it gets,"* said Paul. *"Do you miss your mother, Nate?"*

"Yes I do, more than life itself," said Nate.

"Great choice of words," said Paul. *"Ok here's the thing I have to show you,"*

Paul said. *"Do you remember the story on the news referring to the missing girl in St Paul?"*

"Yeah, I remember. It was broadcasted on the news last night at the restaurant, but this is a freezer, not a girl," Nate said.

Then Paul opened the freezer, *"Here she is, under your date and my date."*

Nate laughed nervously and then sucked it in as he slowly

Dropped to his knees and said, "Why Paul? Why?"

"The funny thing is, I don't know. I must get back to you on that one. Oh wait, you won't be here, but the good thing is that I will be reuniting you with your mom soon," Paul explained.

What?" said Nate?

"No, 'thank you' is what should be coming out of your mouth. Well you're welcome Nate," said Paul as he got near Nate.

"Hey," Nate said, "I'll kick your ass. I'm not a

Female."

"Oh, I've killed men too, bigger than me. So bring it mama's boy, " Paul responded.

"Fuck you, insensitive bastard," said Nate as he swung on Paul but missed. Paul got two jabs in with the knife on Nate's right side.

"Ah shit, that hurt," moaned Nate.

"That's nothing. Wait until I slit your throat tough guy, " Paul said as he

followed a wounded Nate around the basement. *"You should stop and die because I got stuff to do in the event of going back to work tomorrow. I have to make my lunch, do laundry, etc.,"* Paul said.

"You're so cocky," said Nate.

"Nah, just goal orientated," Paul replied. Suddenly, Nate stopped, "Fuck it!!" and raised both of his arms like Christ and said, "Mom I'll be seeing you soon…"

"Hmm, what's cooking?"
Suzy got up and followed
the food smell to the
kitchen.

"Hey, and you can cook
too?" Suzy asked.

"Yes I do," George replied.

"Morning sweetie.
I made breakfast come and
have a seat."

"Damn your marriage
material," Suzy said.

"I guess," replied George.

"This is not a typical
breakfast discussion, but

I'm wondering what's
going on over there"
'George questioned.
"it's like witnessing a fight
at school, it's best to ignore
it and keep on moving,"
"Because if you're nosey,
you can lose your nose,"
said Suzy,
"But what if I call over
there?" asked George.
"You could lose an ear
"joked Suzy
"Ok silly," said George.
"Seriously, you work with
him, right?" She asked.
"Yes, I do. Why?" George

replied.

"Listen to me. Don't ask.
Don't tell. Ignore and
avoid, when you can. Say
you had a nice time. Sorry,
you had to leave because
your mom was sick. Make
something up he doesn't
know what we know, less is
more !!" Suzy said.

"Ok, I will do. But What if
Paul calls me?" asked
George.

"Don't answer, that's why
there's a thing called voice
mail," she said.

"And besides, God is on

our side. So, what're your plans for today?" asked George.

"I don't have any," said Suzy. "I can cuddle with you if you don't mind." George smiled.

"And I owe you big time, one for saving my life, and two for making me breakfast," said Suzy.

"Ah, it was nothing," said George.

"But we both owe my mom. Let's visit her today."

"Sure," agreed Suzy but I must shower first. I have an

extra change of clothes in my car."

"Cool," said George.

They headed downstairs to the car. Things just felt weird as if they were being watched, so they hurried back upstairs after getting her clothes and laughed, "Nobody's after us, "We need to stop that!" Suzy said, "Cool and calm for us from now on."

"Ok, babe," agreed George.

"Shower time," he said.

"Ladies first," said Suzy.

"No problem," said George gallantly.

George walked into his room and got clothes ready for the day.

While Suzy showered, he called his Mom.

Ring, Ring.

"Hello," Mom answered.

"Hey," said George.

"Hey, Georgie,"

"What are you doing Mom today? George asked.

"Um, nothing," Mom replied.

"Do you need anything

from the store," George asked.

"Um, milk and bread and butter," said Mom.

"Ok, if you think of something else give me a call. We're coming over in about an hour," George said.

"Ok, Georgie. Love you," said Mom.

"Love you too Mom. Bye, Bye," said Mom. Click.

George and Suzy got dressed, went to the store and then to his mom's

house. On the way, they
saw someone who
resembled Nate walking
through a cemetery, crying.
George asked Suzy,
"Should I stop?"
She starting crying, "No
don't stop!! Can't you see
that's a sign that's he's
dead, that's his spirit's
roaming for the light?"
"Wow, you're deeply
scaring me," said George.
"I'm sorry, but we have to
stay the course, said Suzy.
"Whew, the hair on the
back of my neck is standing

up," said George.

"Awe," Suzy said. Then she reached over and started rubbing George's neck.

"Ah, you are so comforting to me," he said.

"That's my job and Thanks for acknowledging," said Suzy.

"You're welcome," said George. "We are here babe. Can you grab those bags on your side?"

"Sure," said Suzy. "Aren't you demanding?" she asked.

"Yep, now you know what

it would be like dating me."
George smiled and said,
They both giggled as they
closed the car doors. There
was a significant gust of
wind, as they walked up the
broken concrete stairs.
"I wonder how much
cement it will take to get
her stairs fixed," Suzy said,
"because I know guys that
could do this for next to
nothing."

"That would be great
because I don't want her to
fall," said George.

"Remind me later to call them," said Suzy.

"Ok,"

Suddenly, they felt someone's eyes on them. then George realized it was his mom's eyes piercing through the curtains."

"Open up Momma," said George.

Suzy asked, "You have an extra key in case of emergencies?" "Nope," said George.

"you need me in your life so I can think of things that you need," said Suzy.

George looked Suzy in the
eyes and said, "If you want
me."

"I'm yours for the taking,"

The door opened, and Mom
gave them both a group
hug.

"Ah, I'm so happy that you
guys are alright," Mom
said.

George said to his mom, "If
it weren't for you, we
would not be alive!"

"Come on in and have a
seat," Mom replied.

"I'll put those groceries up," said George.

After that, they sat. And collected themselves after such a stressful night.

Suzy shimmied herself in his arms and said, "Hi, Handsome." They both smiled.

Mom said, "Can I get you guy's anything? A soda, bottled water?"

"Water please," they answered, "thanks, mom."

Chapter 15:
Troubles at home and Work

Officer Nelson sits at his desk wondering what's happening to his city. "Damn, just in the last two months we've had a hand full of missing people, and I got the feeling in my soul that they won't be the last."

Ring.......

"Officer Nelson speaking,"

"Hey, this is John from the 13th precinct,"

"Hey John, Do you got anything for me?" Officer Nelson asked.

"Yes, I do." "We located Amber's car in the impound lot. They towed it on Concord Street after it sat in a no parking zone for two days. We checked it out and dusted for prints. It was mostly her and a guy named Clarence. He was her ex. We're keeping tabs on him and keeping our options open." He replied

"Thanks, John," said Officer Nelson, as a cliché I always feel it can be an ex or a husband. Maybe she wanted to leave because she was unhappy etcetera."

"Most definitely!" John agreed. "I'll keep you posted on any further updates."

"Thanks".

Click.

"So how are you guys holding up?" asked Mom?
"We're ok. I think we saw a ghost

today, I think it was my friend from last night." George explained.

"Yes, it was him," "I felt everything was done by 8 am this morning He was looking for you two, but not anymore, because you're no longer a threat to him for now. But you have to play it cool, especially at work tomorrow. He's going to expect you to ask him about the friend." said Mom.

"Well, I hardly see him except for special cleaning projects," said George.

"Well that works to your advantage," said Mom.

"Yes, it does, "the next time I see him at work, I'm going to thank him for his hospitality, and move on."

"Good," said Suzy.

"So tell me all about last night," said Mom.

"Well, last night was a boy's night out for Nate because he lost his mother a few weeks ago and was sulking in his apartment for days.

Paul just wanted to cheer Nate up. So Nate agreed to go out and have a good time, then Paul called me. I didn't have anything planned, and one thing led to another, and we went to a restaurant and two bars. The last one is where I met Suzy, and we all headed back to Paul's place for a nightcap. I went to the bathroom to check my phone when I saw that you called me numerous times I knew it was an emergency said George,"

"So if I called once you wouldn't have called me back? Asked Mom.

"I was tired, and I probably wouldn't have, but who only calls once if there's an urgency between life and death?" questioned George.

"Good point," Mom said.

"The thing that bugs me is this was supposed to be a good time to uplift Nate's spirit, no pun intended," said George.

"Son, there are Angry Spirits in that house. They were people he killed, and they made one of the guests seek out her remains. That's is what sparked today's events. Mom explained

"Yeah that reminds me, he told us specifically not to go into the basement because it was flooded. said, George.
"NO, it isn't," Mom interrupted. "a girl with the first Initial A is in a cold place in the basement, maybe a freezer." "Maybe we should call the cops, to inspect," George suggested.
"No!" Suzy said.
And mom agreed, "The last thing you want to do is to let him know that you're on to him!!"
"True" I just need to listen said George.   "you got that from your father. God bless his soul, but he was as stubborn as a bull and grabbed his life by the horns.

"On that note, Mom, we have to be going," "I will answer and return all your calls for now on," said George. "Here's my card, just in case," to George's mom Suzy said. "Now you kids be careful now". "Ok, we will," "Thanks again for looking out for us." "No problem, that's my job," said Mom. "Bye," said George and Suzy. "Bye," said Mom.

After the door closed, George's mom started crying as she headed to the Kitchen table.

"Man, I was a busy little boy today. "I killed more before 8 am than most soldiers do in their lifetime". Whew, now what to do? First, I must collect all credentials thought Paul

"Let me go to the extra room first, "

said Paul to himself.

As he went through Nate's pants pockets, he thought, *"Why didn't I get rid of Amber's car? That might come back and bite me. Fuck it! Spilled milk."*

"He gathered the belongings from each room.
He started with the master bedroom "where's her purse.   Damn, what was my date name? I think it was Amy."

Paul dug through the purse and pulled out a wallet inside. *"Hmm, I guess I was right, Oh Amy. Damn, she looks so familiar,* thought Paul. As he continued, he ran into her work I.D at the same time he saw his phone number in her wallet. Paul dropped everything in shock that the girl he killed was the girl at the clothing store that he never called. She was so lonely that she kept his number hoping that he would call. *Maybe she was too scared to call me, or maybe she just hadn't cleaned out her purse. "Yeah maybe it was the latter," thought Paul.*

Bewildered Paul had to figure out how to dispose of the group. *"I have no choice but to dump their bodies in a trash bin then torch the motherfuckers and drive off. Then poof, ten o'clock news. "Thought Paul*

He got a roll of trash bags and laid out some window insulation plastic on the basement floor. He went upstairs to get his meat cleaver, gloves and scissors and went back downstairs. He grabbed one of the black bags and cut three holes in it and slid the bag over his head and stuck his arms out of the side holes. Then got to work dismembering and bagging up his victims. Six pieces of a large bag are how he figured it, two arms, two legs, a head, and torso.

After he had three full bags, he thought, *"Fuck it! Let me get the fourth bag for Amber. That bitch has been bothering my guests and me in recent days. She should be easy because she's frozen I could just snap her into pieces."* Paul said and laughed to himself.

He waited 'til darkness fell before he loaded up his car. *"Ok, it's dark enough out, and we have cleaned the house to the best of our ability,"* he said.
Paul threw his bloody clothes, mop head, and rags in the can in his backyard. He was all packed up and now the search was on to find a big Bin in a deserted area.

As he was driving, he thought, *"Man it would be fucked up to get pulled over. I would rather have drugs on me than this."* He laughed to himself, then he thought, *"Oh yeah, that slaughterhouse on 5ᵗʰ street. Kind of ironic, hmm."*

As Paul turned onto Fifth Street, he checked both ways like someone crossing the street. He parked right next to a dumpster, then got out the car and lifted the lid and tossed the bags from the trunk and backseat into the trash, as well as the towels that were under the bags in case of leakage.

"Ok, all in," said Paul. He started squirting the lighter fluid on the bags, still nervously looking all around the area. Now that the can was empty and it was time for him to light it. *"Oh, Shit! I forgot the matches. You dumb fucker. How could you? Damn leave it to you, and this would happen! Ok, let me close the lid and come right back."* Paul got into the car and shot home.

He left the car running as he went in.

"Got them. Let's hurry up and get back to finish up this shit," thought Paul.

He turned back onto Fifth Street, headed down the block and noticed some man trying to dig through the trash bins on the block. *"Oh shit! He's about to fuck up my plan."* said Paul. As he drove slowly down the block, Paul was hoping that the derelict was going to flee thinking he was a cop. But nope, he was persistent in his search for food or cans.

Paul rolled down his window and in a stern voice said, *"What are you doing?"*

"Minding my own fucking business. What's is it to you?" The derelict answered.

"I guess I can go for five," Paul replied.

"What the fuck does that mean?" said the guy.

Paul informed him, *"You've been selected by the Reaper to separate your soul from your body so you can perish into hell."*

With that, Paul stepped out of the car, and got a pole from his back seat, stuck it down the back of his pants and walked over to the guy who was still looking around. The guy sucker-punched Paul.

Paul shook his head and said, *"Are your parents dead?"*

The guy said, "Yep."

Paul responded, *"Well, a reunion is due,"* then he walked the guy so fast and hit him so hard that the pole dented in his skull about two inches deep.

Paul grabbed him and flipped him into the dumpster, then he struck three matches to make it light up faster. Paul closed the lid, got into his car and sped off. From his rearview mirror, he could see the smoke growing from inside the dumpster. *"Whew,"* he had a deep sigh of relief then cracked a smile when he looked back and saw the flames peeking out of the closed lid.

As he returned home, he quickly thought of what he bought and stored in his glove compartment. "Oh yeah, my home needs some spiritual cleansing," said Paul as he grabbed the sage. Heading into the house, he started to light the match, *"Damn these matches suck. I can't get a light."* He tried the lighter and still no success. He smiled and said, *"I get it,"* so he walked outside and then the lighter worked. He got the sage smoking. Then walked around the outside then went inside. He went to the basement first, walked around, headed upstairs and went to every room 'til he felt it was cleansed. Then put the sage out in the kitchen sink.

"Oh shit. I haven't checked my phone," said Paul. As he checked his phone, he had a couple missed phone calls from Jane and six texts, one from Jane and four from that weird number again.

Paul first looked at Jane's, "Hey babe how did your night go with the guys? Call me when you get the chance. Not in a lovey-dovey mood?"

Next text, from the weird number: "Hey I just got the hang of this."

"Huh?" said Paul.

Next text, from the weird number again: "I'm going to let her know about it."

"Who the hell is this?" questioned

Paul.

Next text: "She's my little puppet, and I'm leading her to me."

"Damn! I need to change my number," thought Paul.

Next text: "Oh you brought me, friends. Strength in numbers."

Anyway, next text: "I'm not in the freezer no more. Oh, wait. It's kind of hot. I'm burning! Let me out! Help! What did I do? Help!"

"Huh? Creepy, but as I stated, 'Anyway.'" said Paul. He deleted all his text messages and then prepared for his shower.

"Damn, tomorrow work. I hate my boss. I hate working. I wish I was rich and didn't have to work anymore. I think I'm the only one in the world with those feelings," Paul

sarcastically said and laughed then got his underwear, and pajamas out of his drawer.

As Paul walked into the bathroom, he heard his phone start ringing. *"Fuck that! When I'm busy, I'm busy, leave a message."* Then he cut the shower on, disrobed and got in.

"All this angst has to leave me," he thought. *"If there is a God, hopefully, He'll forgive me because I had no choice but to commit malice. They were going to tell, and I love my freedom. Ever since I left my family, I knew that I was never going to submit ever again. Well, my wife, hmm, and my boss. Oh, fuck it! No more now! I mean it,"* said Paul out loud. He finished his shower without incident, crawled into bed, and quickly fell asleep. Paul felt he had a tough day and evening, *"Full-time janitor, part-time killer, only paid for the*

one." Poor old Me.

As morning came, he felt refreshed, youthful like a child who had the summer off from school. He stretched as he got out of bed and thought of breakfast. *"Hmm, do I want to make it or go out for it? Fuck it! I feel good. Let's make someone else make my breakfast for me. I should have Jane meet me. Let me text her."*

"Hey, babe let's meet at pancake plaza in an hour for breakfast. My treat, Paul." Send.

"What should I wear? Shit, sweats and a t-shirt and sandals," said Paul to himself. As he got his clothes on his phone went off. Beep ….. Beep.
"Oh, that's my sweetie. Let me see what time we are meeting."

Paul opened his phone and saw a

message from Jane in large print that read, "FUCK YOU!!!"

Paul frantically messaged back, "What's wrong sorry I didn't get back to you yesterday I was busy." Paul's heart started beating fast as he was misspelling a lot of the words trying to explain "Hey, why did you text him that? What did I tell you? 'Do not get angry or lead him to believe you're on to him.' What did he say in response?" asked the Officer.

"Sorry for that," said Jane. Anyway, he was just all apologetic. So, no harm is done. Should I meet him for breakfast?"

"Yes you should but let me call the captain to set up surveillance for you if you want to do this," the Officer replied.

"Yes I'll do it," said Jane, "and I'll

do whatever it takes to find out the information on the disappearance of my brother and others. And if I find that Paul was in any shape or form involved with it, after trying to date me, I will kill him two times, once for the body and again for the soul," Jane claimed.

"When I would hate to be that guy, mmm-hmm," said one of the officers.

"So text him and say you're sorry, sometimes you get a temper and can get a little jealous," advised the Officer.
"Done," said Jane.
Jane texted Paul, "Let's meet in an hour." Send.
Paul got happy, "Ok sweetie an hour Muah XOXO." "Muah to back to you too OXOX☺," replied Jane.
"Yuck, it's hard being falsely sweet," said Jane to the Officer.
"Well, it's just for the

investigation," the Officer assured her.

"Ok, Sir," said Jane.

Officer Daniel showed up moments later with the equipment. "Ok let me strap the wire on the subject, and then we'll do a quick test for sound," said Officer Daniel. How long 'til the meeting."

"25 minutes and counting," said the First Officer.

Ok, we will be ready in 7," said Officer Daniel.

"Ok, it's connected. You may talk Jane for a mic reading."

"Ok. Testing one, two, three," said Jane. "I'm the dopest female MC." Everyone started laughing, Jane said, "What's funny? I'm serious," then she cracked a smile. "Ok, let's do this."

"There will be an agent right across the street," explained the Officer, "and our safe word is Curry."

"Why do we need a safe word? Are we performing S&M?" Jane quipped.

"Aren't you full of jokes today, Miss?" the Officer replied.

"Nah," said Jane. "I'm just making light of the matter so I won't crack."

"It's going to be ok. We will prevail, if not sooner, then later, but we will," the Officer assured Jane.

"Ok, I will have more faith in you," said Jane with tears in her eyes.

As she left to get in her car, the officers left to their designated post. Minutes later Jane pulled up and went into the Pancake Plaza.

"Hello, welcome to the Pancake Plaza," said the hostess greeting Jane.

"I'm here to meet someone," explained Jane.

"What's the name?" asked the hostess.

"Paul Nelson," said Jane.

"We don't have anyone with that name listed, you must have beat him here. I'll get you a table for two," replied the hostess.

"Ok," said Jane. "Oh, Can I get one by the window facing south?"

"Sure, right over here." said the hostess.

"Ok, thanks," Jane responded.

"No problem," said the hostess. "I'll grab you two menus."

"Thanks," as she grabbed her cell phone out of her purse, and texted the officers, "He's not here yet, but I got a window seat, said, Jane."

Then she texted Paul, "Where are you?"

Buzz......... Buzz "Ok that was quick thinking being by the window," replied the Officer "Make sure you delete all of our texts," the Officer texted.

"Done and Done," Jane texted back.

As she was deleting the messages, Paul walked in and waited to be seated.

"Hello I supposed to meet someone here," Jane heard from afar.
Jane saw Paul, but he didn't see her, so she texted the Officers, "He's here now, Jane." Then she deleted the text in seconds and put the phone back into her purse before Paul laid eyes on her.

"Hey sweetie," said Paul as he approached the table.
"Hey," Jane replied with a fake smile.
"Can I get a hug?" He asked.
"Not yet," said Jane. "I'm still mad at you."
"Well, I can make it all better, if we go to my house after breakfast,"
"Well, we will see," replied Jane.

"Did you decide what you wanted, because you were here before me and I figured you had time to do so?" questioned Paul.

"Well, you figured wrong as men are known to do, but the truth is that I was courteous, so we could order together," she said and smiled.

"Awe, thanks, sweetie," Paul said appreciatively.

"You're welcome, man," said Jane. Then they ordered their food.

"What could I have done to deserve an F-Bomb via text?" Paul asked

"I told you I can be a Bitch sometimes!" said Jane.

"And I said I was sorry, so let's move on."

Jane paused. "So what's new with you and what did you guys do last night? Asked Jane with a calculated grin.

"Nothing much, the basic guy's night out stuff, dinner, strip bar and a regular bar that's it," Paul

replied.

"Hmm," said Jane. "I don't know, seems like it was more, but I wasn't there so I can't say."

"Here's your food," said the waitress as she set the meals down. Paul looked a little nervous, so Jane asked him, "What's wrong?"
"Oh, nothing, just that I'm hungry and I don't want to go to work," Paul replied.
"Oh poor baby," teased Jane as Paul placed his napkin on his lap.
Jane plowed right into the food like she had the appetite of ten men.

Paul thought, *"Wow if we get married she's going to carry me across the threshold."*

Then, suddenly, Jane stared at Paul and started choking as if something went down the wrong pipe. As she choked, louder everyone began to stare. Then Jane turned red, and a guy quickly got up and said, "I know the Heimlich Maneuver," and he ran behind Jane and started. Paul just sat back and watched helplessly. Then the food came out of her mouth. Jane sighed with relief and stood up. The bug must have unraveled in the process of the Heimlich, and it dropped to the floor. Paul quickly slipped out of the restaurant after seeing the device. Jane sat down realizing, not only had she blown the surveillance, but she also got stuck with the bill.

Paul drove home in a frenzy and just blew up screaming, *"THAT FUCKING BITCH "THEY'RE GOING TO COME TO MY HOUSE AND ARREST ME. OH, FUCK!!!!"* He broke mirrors and windows, smashed chairs against the walls.

After calming down, he started packing a bag for work, knowing that he probably was not going to return home. He spent most of the time peeking out the window waiting until it would be time to leave for work. Every car that drove by was suspect in his eyes and if they slowed down or parked he damn near pissed his pants in fear.

"I can try to live at work," he reasoned. *"Just go to the bathroom at 8:30 and stay until 11:00 PM. When security leaves for the night, we can move around and go to the vending machine and shower, until we find out our next move."*

Paul looked at his watch and saw that it was time for work. Knowing that his bag was packed, he quickly ran to his bedroom to the dresser and pulled out the bottom drawer and pulled out five hundred dollars he was saving. Paul stood up, looked around the living room, took a deep breath and exhaled with a tear in his eyes and said, *"Oh man, this was my home. I messed up. I messed up really bad, and it can't be fixed.*" Paul flung his bag over his shoulder, got the keys and stepped out into an uncertain world. He put his bag into the trunk, got into the car and drove to work.

Ten minutes later an unmarked police vehicle pulled up in front of Paul's home. Two cops got out of the car, walked to the door and started knocking hard.
Boom Boom!!
"Hello. Mr. Nelson. It's the Saint Paul Police Department. Open up."
Boom Boom Boom.

"What are you doing?" asked the first Officer, Officer Nelson, pulled out his wallet and took out a credit card.
"Don't even think about it!!" the Officer warned.
"We have a warrant being produced as we speak.   So,

if we wait for just a little, then we can comb the house for any evidence. Right now, he's just a person of interest."

"If that were the case, he would have stayed instead of fleeing after the wire fell," said Officer Nelson. "Wait a minute, isn't this guy your brother?" asked the First Officer

"Oh yeah, but the law is the law, and besides we didn't get along anyway," said Officer Nelson.

"Why?" asked the other Officer.

"It's a long story," replied Officer Nelson. "You know, the middle child syndrome. The baby is the favorite, and the oldest is the boldest to hold it all together, so on and so on. We weren't the nicest to him, but we were kids following the direction of our parents. After he moved out, I felt bad about it all and started to miss him. The others might have as well. I don't know. I haven't kept in touch all that much, except for the holidays."

"Anyway, what's taking them so long with the warrant? The suspense is giving me gas," complained Officer Nelson.
"Nah I think it's the bean and cheese burrito we had for lunch," his partner replied
"Ha ha."
As they laughed, as the Captain pulled up with the papers. Thanks, said Nelson.

We need two at the back door, and we will let you in afterward.
Knock Knock "We have a warrant to enter the premises," announced the Officers.
After 1 minute with no answer, they kicked down the door.
Boom.
With their guns drawn, the officers slowly entered the home of Paul Nelson. They started searching throughout the house when they discovered all kinds of orange spots on the carpet, holes in the walls,

broken windows and mirrors. and broken chairs.

"He probably did this damage after the wire dropped," said Officer Nelson. "He knew he was a suspect and freaked out. That's why he's not home now.

"I agree," said the Officers.

Hours went by as they combed the house for evidence and the forensics team took DNA samples. They finally made it to the basement, and all the Officers were on edge as to what they would find.

One of the Officers said, "I've seen a lot of fucked up shit, for instance, the Miller case."

Another Officer interrupted him.

"You worked on that one?"

"Yes, I did, and I should have retired after that one, even though I was only thirty," said the Officer.

The other Officer replied, "Damn,

sorry."

He continued, "Yep, that man killed his whole family, from his wife to his seven children. What did a three-year-old do to deserve to be murdered?"

Another Officer shook his head in disbelief as they walked down the stairs and cut the light on. "Ah, good nobodies so far. Whew!"

The second Officer said, "I can never get used to this. No matter what I walk into, body parts, puddles of blood, brains, you name it, it's always new to me."

One Officer said, "Damn, this basement is clean. He must know what he's doing. I guess he got sloppy upstairs, with the spots and all. Let's open this freezer.

The second Officer quipped, "Ah shit, here we go, bodies in the freezer scenario. Huh? Nothing."

"Wait to shine your flashlight over here in this corner," said the first Officer.

"Ok," the second Officer replied. "More blood, huh."

Radio-static … "Officers near Arcade and Fourth Street. We have a Multiple 187. Bodies found burnt in a dumpster near Fifth and Arcade."
  "We're on our way" the Captain responded to Dispatch.   He directed the Officers, "Let's head out guys. I'll tell the forensic team to check those spots and swab the freezer as well."
"Ok Sir," they responded.

They arrived at the scene of the dumpster, and walked over and looked in. "Oh shit, that's gross. Looks like a BBQ of smoked bodies. Damn! This will be a bad day for the coroner. Please Give them a call," said the Captain.

Paul was hard at work, he told himself, *"It's going to be alright.*

They don't have anything on me. Yep, I should be able to go home and live comfortably, and no more killing, I swear on my Wife no more!"

Hours later Paul finished his shift. *"I think I should leave my bag in my closet, until tomorrow. Let me head home and see how the situation is"* thought Paul.

On his way to the door, Paul told the guard, *"I must run home for a second, and I might need to come back for a late job for Jolene."*

"Ok, I'm here until eleven," the guard replied.

Paul got into his car and drove home, his house lights was on, and a woman was on his front porch wearing a Tyvek suit and smoking a cigarette. He knew it was over, he headed back to work with the empty feeling that the end was near.

Chapter 16:
The Clearance, everyone must go.

Ding Dong ……….. Ding Dong, HOLD ON, Damn, who could be at our door at this time? I don't know but check it out Howie, Ok Hun. Yes, may I help you? A muffled voice responded, *"Hey it's Paul,"* Oh Hold on a second, Howard whispered to his Wife "It's Paul," we haven't heard from him in years, let him in.

Are we're going to start being nice now? Better late than never Paul's mother said, He grunted as he walked to the door and opened it. Hey Paul, how's it going? *Not good* as he walked past his father and sat down. So, what's new? Asked Mom, *Well Stacey*

*left me over a month ago
with a guy. I think he was
the Devil or a Saint I don't
know.* Sorry, I knew she was
not good for you.
*Well, you could have said
something before I married
her,* you seemed happy, and
I didn't want to intervene
Mom said. *Well the butcher
didn't cry over spilled
Blood, and neither should I,*
Paul explained. So, do you
have a job? If you don't
mind me asking? Said the
father. *I have a job, I'm a
master of the custodial arts.*
That's a fancy word for
Janitor Explained mom,
Paul shrugged his shoulders
and frowned. So, what did
we earn this visit from you
at this hour? *Well, I needed
to talk to someone and have
a place to crash for the*

night, Paul said. What happened to your home? Said the Father.

Well, sometimes a person needs a temporary comfort zone when they feel bad or have some problems to sort out said, Paul. Well, I'm not much of an advice giver, all I can say is put your best foot forward and keep your nose clean, that's all I got, that was the advice given to me as a kid the Father explains. Well, I can get you some pillows and sheets for the sofa. Your Siblings took all the Extra bedding with them when they moved out years ago.

It's been a long time since we had a guest that stayed the night Mother said.

Well, thanks, mom, I really needed this, I hope you're

not in trouble? Asked Paul's father

All we need is the police busting down our door in the wee hours of the night taking us to jail for harboring a criminal. Paul rolled his eyes as he took the potshots from his father assuming things that were strangely true. *Thanks again for letting me stay over said Paul,* Just for one night only!!! All we need is someone trying to take advantage of our generosity, once a bird leaves the nest they can't return said, Howard.

Trust me I don't want to come back and live here! After all, I've been put through enough as a child, made me into the man I am today, and there was a lot to

be desired and feared said,
Paul. Yeah, Yeah Goodnight
Paul said the father with a
smirk splashed across his
face, then retired to the
bedroom, Paul cut off the
lights and laid down on the
couch. One thing Paul never
liked was a quiet house he
always kept the T.V on, and
in his mind, the television
noise drowns out any Ghost
or unsettled house creeks.

So, he just laid there still in
silence knowing that every
sound is going to keep him
awake from the drips in the
sink to any outside noise
wondering is it inside or
out. Paul started tearing up,
all those feelings as a child
came rushing back in a
matter of minutes but it all
went away as he felt

forgivable because they
open the door for him in his
time of need, then after an
hour, Paul fell asleep.
Seven Hours later Paul was
awakened not by noise but
the scent of something
cooking, then the clanking
of dishes being pulled out of
the cupboard, so he opens
his eyes to the light, then he
rose up unraveling the
sheets from around him, he
yarned then rubbed his eyes
and said *good morning.*
Yum said the father,
morning Paul from the
mother. *That was the best
sleep I had in a long while,*
you are leaving today got
that!! Said Howard, *I got it
Geeze.   I'll split
from here and go straight to
work,* Said Paul,
yes you will respond the

father, and I don't
appreciate your tone Mr. we
did you a favor, *Yes you did,
and I thank you dearly!!*

Ok, that's enough talking
let's have breakfast as a
family, *Ok Mom let me use
the restroom first.* Ok, Paul,
we'll begin eating, and
you'll have the purple plate,
ok thanks. The Father
waited till the bathroom
door close to talk about
Paul. You don't have to be
so kind to him, your sugary
mothering disposition is
making me sick before the
syrup hit the pancakes.

Hey, we need to be nicer!!
We weren't the best parents
to him then, but we need to

turn it around before we get old and Die, it's called repentance said the mother, well were already old Fuck it!! Shot back the Father, well you can keep it up, but I won't anymore, so have that with your pancakes Mr. Frumpy grumpy, said Mother. The father smiled and said I love you, you have always been my yin to my yang, ah I love you too Honey, Paul stood there and said *G.A.R, huh* said the mom *"Get a Room,"* said Paul then she laughed. We Have a House and rooms. What do you have? Smartass said the father. *I have a house too it's just being Fumigated for bugs That's why I had to stay last night,* explained Paul. Ok That's cool, I remember when we had to do that a couple years ago, but we went to a hotel stated Father. *We'll let me get started on breakfast since you had a head start on me, Hmm this looks good mom thanks,* you 're welcome my son.

Hey, I paid for the food claimed the father, *thank you as well,* said Paul. Then he started to eat for the first time at this table without sneaking and stress, *um this is delicious, I can't remember home cooking,* what about Stacey did she cook for you? *No, she just was too busy cheating, so I had to make my own dinner, or pick things up on my way home.* Oh poor baby Said Mom, it will be ok said the father, and Paul smiled......

Honk......Honk Paul awakens in the back seat of his car parked close to his job, *I knew it was too good to be true.* Paul looked at his watch and said *damn it's too early to go in. It would be too hot. I need to sneak in when security is doing their rounds, they might have cut my access off.*

He climbed into the front seat then looked around before turning the ignition then pulled out. *I'm hungry let's get some breakfast, that dream was too real, I could even taste the pancakes. Shit my picture could be on the news, hmm better be discreet about this* Paul thought as he dug in his glove compartment and pulled out some sunglasses, then he saw a beat-up hat in the back seat then slapped that on. Paul knew of this hole in the wall diner off Barley Street, where you can get a full breakfast for $5.99 and refills of any beverages you want for free.

He pulls into the parking lot, then headed in. Table *for one, please.* The waitress led him to his table, *oh can I get a table by the window because I lack Vitamin D,* But its cloudy sir, *I heard the sun was coming out later* interjected Paul, ok here's your seat and menu I'll be back in a minute to take your order said the waitress, *Thanks.*

He thumbed through the menu, *too filling, um not*

enough, ok that's it unlimited pancakes, with one side order, add a drink for a dollar perfect, I'm ready. Paul gave his order, then checked his phone for any incriminating texts and deleted them, then looking out the window wishing his life was different and dwelling on his current plans. Five minutes later breakfast came and started grubbing down, as his worries and regrets took the backseat to his appetite. Then suddenly, a cop comes in the diner asking the owner can he place some flyers on the bulletin board, the owner wasn't there, so the cashier agreed as the officer pulled them out of his folder, Paul turned around for a sec then quickly turned back. Oh, shit whispered then lowered his head close to his plate as taking little bites of his food chewing softly as to hear everything the cop was saying. Peeking from time to time to see what he does. *Hmm, he's probably about to put up pictures of me* said, Paul, as he was peeking over his shoulder, *oh that's not even a good picture of me, the sketch artist probably was drunk when he or she drew that. I got to find a window of opportunity to get out of here,* said Paul. Hey where's the restroom

Asked the cop, around the back I'll show you said the Hostess, as they walked off, Paul quickly threw his money down for the food and service and ran to the front counter and grabbed his folder of flyers and ran out of the diner before the cop returned. Into the trash they went, then he jumped in his car and sped off.

Man, oh man I must find a way to sneak into work tonight because I have no options and no place to stay, the walls of life, are closing in on me, I shake my head in shame, though I am still that little boy who was never giving love, care or respect only to deal with neglect Thought Paul.

He parked a block away from his job, so he can stay at bay and get a good view of the comings and goings of the building. As time ticked on Paul waited patiently, not even to go to the restroom, he had a couple of empty water bottles, so he wouldn't leave his post. As night fell, and most employees were gone home then saw the security guard walking around and was locking up the gate.   Paul got out of the car and ran to the building and placed his I.D card against the reader "Beep Beep" *Ah Fuck!* Said, Paul, as he tugged on the door handle. *They must have cut my access off,* "Beep Beep" *shit* as he tried again, So Paul Stayed At the door to see if someone is going to leave or enter the building because some employees would let him in not knowing the details of the events of the cleaners.

Damn I must get my bag and shelter it's starting to get a little chilly out here, and I must take a wicked Two. Minutes later Paul heard rubber rolling on the asphalt and turned slowly and there where a guy getting out of his car and slowly approaching the building and Paul remembered there is a 10-second unlocking rule of the door. Once someone scans the reader that have access, so he knew he had to be quick about it, so he got in his stance and was ready to run to the door.

"Beep Beep" Click as the guy scanned his card then opened the door   Paul shot to the door in seconds then fake scanned his card so it can look like he had had access to the building as well. *Hello*, Said Paul, *I left my bag in the building after my shift*, hmm said the guy, *I'm a janitor* said Paul, oh that must be nice said the guy as he got on the elevator with him, *what floor do you need?* Fourth said the guy then Paul pressed four and five.

Ding *"Have a good evening."* Paul said, in which nothing was said in return as he got off the elevator. So *fucking rude* said Paul under his breath as the door closes. Ding the elevator hit the fifth floor He stuck his head out of the car looked both ways for people or security, he saw nothing then stepped out and walked to his closet and opened the door and saw nothing but the garbage barrel, mop, broom, and vacuum. Paul held in his anger as his tote containing clothes, snacks and knife were gone.

So, he closed and locked the door from the inside and sat down in the closet is as quiet as a mouse till his watch struck midnight. Beep his watch alerted the twelve o' clock hour so he came out the closet making sure he unlocks the door, so he can return.

It was dark on the floor kind in a spooky way that would have scared most people. Paul slowly walked down the halls to the bathroom. Then he emerged later feeling refreshed then went to the vending machine to get late-night snacks.

After he was done Munching, he had to find a place to hide during the day and evenings. So, Paul went to the bathrooms to look for vents and air ducts that he could quickly enter and exit and found none till he was leaving the bathroom and saw a little door with a latch behind the bathroom door.

Let's see where this leads to, Paul opened the door saying *I'm glad that I'm small, so I can fit in* here, he climbed in to see how much room he has. After jumping in, he placed his wallet to keep the door ajar. *This is kind of snug, but I can manage. Paul* crawled out of the space to check and see if the other bathrooms were equipped with the hidden area.
Down the stairwell to check each bathroom for the hiding space compartment. With no luck, knowing that was the only one, he ventured to the lower level floor so he can take a shower before his nap in the

closet before five. At five
the maintenance and
security shows up., Paul
thought of getting some
weapons to protect himself
against anyone he ran into
during his nightly routine
after he bathes. So, he got a
bag and started looking
through people's desk for
anything that can help his
cause, Scissors, letter
openers, T-Pens then Paul
remembered the blades he
would use for the grout he
would scrape off the floors
before waxing.
So ecstatic in collecting
stuff for his arsenal. Didn't
even sleep a wink, *why
sleep now I can sleep in the
space at 4:30 am* he
thought. Suddenly 4:15
came, he said *well I better
get this stuff to the spot so I*

can sleep.

Paul climbed in the cubby hole for hibernation. Then minutes later he had heard the first noises, so he laid still as people ran in and out of the bathroom, then it hit him, He was getting light headed what's wrong with me? He said to himself, *shit I'm dying in this hole, I guess this is how it will end. Would anybody care? Fuck no!! Why should they? Shit, I need Air!!*

I need to prop this open. Paul stuck his finger out to prop it open a tiny bit so the oxygen can stimulate his lungs and brain, *what could*

I use? My wallet it's too thick, ah let me see, um I can use my watch band, so I can get just enough air and have the light when needed.

At 4:30 PM a voice like no other woke him up, *I guess she's cleaning the bathrooms today* thought Paul. "Yeah, I had to let one of my janitors go, his lazy ass didn't even show up for work, and he had the nerves to have The Police sniffing around here" A Loud "Why" squeaked through Jolene's phone. They wouldn't say as she continued to berate Paul. Yeah, I never liked him. He had a fucked up attitude, and Paul smelled as well, geese have you ever heard of Soap, water, and

deodorant, I should have
been fired his ass, but Larry
wanted to keep him, I
should have terminated both
of their asses, then laughter
broke out. Yep, I have to
clean these bathrooms all
week long so I will be
calling you again tomorrow
girl at the same time same
shitty place. That's' all Paul
needed to hear with anger
and dust in his eyes. As time
went on, he thought of
nothing but retaliation, so
he laid and waited till
twelve and climbed out then
looked in the mirror. He
looked like he worked in a
coal mine, and said *I'm
breathing this shit in*, so he
knew where to find one of
those air masks

The next day people came

and went, and all Paul thought about was when will 4:30 get here. The traffic in the bathroom died down, he got out and hid in one of the stalls and waited. She was late, but indeed she came in talking with her cell phone locked between her ear and shoulder.

Didn't even bother to knock to see if someone was in the bathroom or prop the door open for courtesy. Jolene started cleaning the sinks and talking about people.

"I don't care about these janitors"!

Except when they slave and pay for our home, cars and our lavish vacations then I say thanks for your hard work jerks."

So attentive in cleaning the
sinks and her phone
conversation she didn't
notice Paul sneak out from
the stall behind her then she
quickly looked up right
before he knocked her out.

Then he stuffed her in a
bag then place it in the front
compartment of the mop
bucket cart and through a
bag of trash over her
because he had something
special in store for her. He
finished her job cleaning the
bathrooms, he ran into some
co-workers hey Paul you're
back? *"Yeah just had to take
care of some-things"* as he
pushes the cart around with
trash on top of his
unconscious boss, then on
his last floor, he ran into
George, Paul?? Hey, I

thought she fired you, said George, *she did, but I fired her* Paul said under his breath, *huh oh nothing it's good to be back,* well it's good to have you back Paul said to George as he walked off with a puzzled looked on his face. Then turned the corner and then called 911." Hello, what is your emergency", Hi my name is George the guy you were looking for yesterday is here in the building cleaning today, Hold on I will transfer you, said the operator, Ok George whispered.

Paul walked on the dock with his cart then through his trash in the big bend, then throwing the bag with Jolene into the cardboard bailer compressor. He closed the gate tap, tap, and tap on the gate with a broomstick. *Wake up big mouth, I know you can hear* me. Then moans and the rustling of the bag in a dazed tone she spoke, where am I? Ring…. Ring…. Ring as her cellphone sounded off Paul Smiled and pushed the button then suddenly, she knew where she was. HELP!!!! At the top of her lungs then she gasped to scream again but it was too late. The steel had compressed her head into her chest. A distorted ringtone was the last sound besides the gears. *Oh, shit* said, Paul, as the blood came gushing out of the holes of the bailer. He quickly mopped up the blood with the speed of a pro like the people who clean up a sweat during a basketball game.

Then Paul got on the elevator to return the cart to the closet. At the same time, he heard police sirens and a helicopter above, so he ran to the stairwell to make a mad dash to his hiding spot. Walking down to the fifth floor, He heard loud footsteps running up the stairs, so he was extra careful to not let the door of the stairwell slam to draw attention.

As he ran to the bathroom and slid into his cubby, he thought to himself *no air for a little while until they check the bathroom.* He got a mask out of his bag and strapped it on and took a deep breath. Not even a minute later he heard the bathroom door fling open, two officers stepped in with their guns drawn then after 20 seconds one said clear, then they were gone. But Paul wasn't born yesterday. so he waited a couple more minutes before putting his watch back in place to vent his new home. Paul began to wonder who tipped them off. *How did the cops show up so fast? It was right after I talked to…. Oh shit* "*George ratted me out,*" *he was with us at the bar, and at my home, the news probably reported about the girls and Nate damn how I could have been so……… you're so stupid, dumb,*

dumb ass fucker Paul said to himself. Then he started tearing up, *I had a home, I had a wife even though she was a whore, but at least I had a life, now I'm stuck in a dirty, smelly hole in a bathroom hiding like a scared little animal.*

I can't do this anymore tomorrow should be the end of everything, and I'm going out with a bang!!! And oh yeah.... I'm coming for you George! Said Paul, before he went to sleep.
Hours later he heard some office workers talking did you know there was a killer in the building? And the cops couldn't find anyone, and that maintenance woman came up missing as well.

Oh yeah, the blonde with the big mouth. That's not a loss, oh you're really mean bob. What??, Paul smiled as he laid in filth for another hour then he had to get out and sit in the stall because his muscles were locking up and needed to stretch. So he climbed out then grabbing his bag limping to the closest stall to the wall and sat there, pondering what's his next move and thinking of his childhood. (Rewind)

Hey Paul, we had an accident in the bathroom, and it has your name written all over it, Laughter broke out between the siblings, that was a good one, hurry up and clean it, shitty boy!! Guess what Paul? You clean good. So good that you should be a janitor when you grow up. Yeah, another sibling agrees so you can clean up other people's poo too, childish laughter burst louder than before, as those embarrassing memories Which led him to think about his wife laughing at him arguing back on what he used to believe in "love and communication" Bullshit!!! His wife told him the too V's is what gets me through tolerating you. Valiums and Vicodin, Oh yeah and S.O.D= some other dick. All her responses to him came all in a row, not tonight I have a headache, You're weak, You're not a man, You can't Fuck, You Have a little Dick. You should have been aborted, Ugh You're stupid, Ugh You're Ugly, You're worthless….. That last word echoed in his head, then tears fell from his eye, as his head slumped, then he raised his head with an evil grin as two more office workers walked in the bathroom and stood at the sink discussing the upcoming football game.

Yeah, I can't wait for the game, said one worker. Hmm don't really care who wins it doesn't change our situation of having to come in here day in and day out slaving away for our bosses, I wish that we would be that lucky that we wouldn't have to come back to this motherfucker said the other guy.

Yep with our luck, it would probably won't be the lottery but death. As they laughed, Paul slipped out of the stall and started laughing with them. Then one of the workers stopped laughing then looked at the other worker with he's crazy expression.but they didn't pay him no mind as he placed a door stopper under restroom door as they used the urinals. As the streams of piss hit the porcelain, one spoke they are you and the misses still having marital problems?

Ugh, then a voice answered *yeah we were, but I took care of it* a slight pause. *"I murdered my wife in cold* *blood with her Friend".*Haha yeah, right then he looked down from looking straight ahead and seen piss all on the floor damn you missed the mark as he slowly looked behind himself as he saw his co-worker on the floor. Lying on the floor in a pool of blood and piss. Oh shit, he whispered as he zipped up his pants and ran to the door. *You forgot to wash your hands* said Paul, as he tugged on the door two times before Paul jabbed a letter opener through the guy's neck and said *well at least tomorrow you don't have work either, and you're welcome* said Paul with a smile.

He stacked the two bodies

in the stall then locked it, then slid under to the next one to escape then grabbed some paper towels to clean the blood then washed up then uncorked the doorstopper then stuck his head out of the bathroom to see what activities were in progress. *Hmm, I should stake out in the women's restroom because they have more stalls, but the ladies are screamers though, and that's a negative.* Then he walked to the closet with the confidence of nothing being wrong and no one paid him any mind.

"I need weapons," shit it's almost starting time, hey this cleaner left their jacket let's check the pockets, he

found gum, candy, and a bus transfer, then he felt the weight from the inside pocket.
Too light for a gun, oh would you look at this, a pocket knife, how convenient, I have an idea, I can take one object and make it to another, so I can have two weapons.

Paul took a mop handle and started carving it at the end so It can puncture like a spear. *This is going to be messy, and for the first time, I don't have to clean up after myself* said Paul, as he continued shaping up the mop stick he saw this chemical that works like chloroform, as he thought back that his boss reminded them to always wear a mask when using it.

Knowing that Paul crammed the bottle in his pocket, and said to himself, *this could come in handy.* Paul bagged up all the other things that could kill people. Then all of a sudden he heard talking about Fifty feet away. *Must be one of the girls that cleans this floor.* Paul got a plastic bag and busted the light bulb in the closet then got behind the door and waited. As the *talking* got louder he got into his stance, then he saw the knob turn, then it stopped the two ladies kept talking, and Paul whispered to himself *come on already shit*, then the knob turned again when he got ready, then it stopped.

You must be kidding me thought Paul. *"One more time and I'll kill them both" I got nothing to lose!!* Then the door opened. She came in the closet clicking the light switch. Huh, that's weird, guess I'll have to leave a note for maintenance then turned in the dark feeling for the trash barrel then Paul threw a bag over her head so she couldn't yell, and snapped her neck until she stopped moving.

He dumped her head first into the trash barrel that her legs flung over the top, then suddenly the door flew opened again, then the voice called Kim are you in here, that was all she said because Paul impaled her in the neck with the mop stick then put her head first in the sink. He put his foot on her head to remove the rod.

"Damn a human kabob," he said.

Paul grabbed a large bag and started trashing the floor, dirty and bloodstained. He began emptying cans dragging his sack around and then was asked by one of the workers where's, is your barrel? *Somebody stole it, but the job must be done explained Paul.* Well, that's dedication carry on sir, *Thanks* said Paul, as he walked to the next cubical, he saw the worker looking at porn on his computer, huh whatever floats your boat. Then he notices the age of the person on the screen was young, very young so Paul saw a drink on his desk and spilled it on him, *Oh I'm so sorry sir* said, Paul

You Fucking idiot how could you be so clumsy. *Sir, I said I was sorry, let me help you. I have something in my closet that would get that stain out in a jiffy* Said, Paul. Ugh, the worker grunted as he clicks to lock his computer and got up and followed behind Paul, *oh could you wait in the bathroom, while I grab the solution from the closet* ?, Yeah answered the worker, as Paul went into the room the worker walked into the bathroom. Oh, might as well take a wiz while I wait for that clumsy asshole. Ah as his stream misted, he heard the door opened, give me a second and I'll be done.

As the guy looked straight ahead suddenly he felt a sting in his throat then saw blood spayed on the wall, and then he collapses. Paul stood over him and *said you're done, scum of the earth, and that's coming from a killer.* Then Paul dragged him into a stall and locked it as Paul continued trashing. He got his fair shares of stares as he finished trashing and recycling, as he got into the elevator and only thought of getting even with George. As the numbers counted down, he plotted his plans. Ding the main floor, the elevator stopped and opened, and Paul walked out slowly and had a swag like a cowboy in the old west, with an I don't give a damn attitude.

He carried the trash to the dock, then placed it the dumpster, and out of his ears, he heard laughter from a distance that sparked his interest, it was George coming to the dock with another co-worker. So, Paul jumped into the large dumpster, then covered himself up with the sacks of trash and laid still.

Hey, you got all the supplies for stripping the dock? Asked George.   We have everything Doug answered. The guys started the preparation for the job, George laid down the stripper, as Doug attached the hose to the wet vacuum and plugged it in and says ready on my end. George screwed the block with nubs then put the scrubbing pad on, propped up the rotary.

Oh, I forgot the blade for the corners, I'll be back it's in the security drawer at another building said, George. As he left, Doug stood patiently holding the wand for the Vacuum. Paul heard George go and then climbed out of the trash bend. George arrived at the other building.

Hey to the security guard, hey what's up, nothing but work George replied, do you want to share my lunch asked the guard with a smile, well what are you having? Asked George, Squirrel and fish heads. Ugh no thank you can have it all, and went behind the desk to get the blade, as he pulled the keys out of his pocket, he looked up and saw the guard waving the squirrel leg in his face. Hey cut it out, stop that shit, gross dude said George, as he got the blade, back up or I'll cut you George joked. So, what are you working on? Doug and I are stripping the dock in the other building, I must hurry back, he's waiting for me, and the floor is drying, alright see you, ok see you. As George was walking down the long corridor he felt a strange sinking feeling

then suddenly his cell phone
rang "Hello" oh Gorgy I
love you, I love you too
Mom, you must promise me
one thing before I Die.......
Is to be careful, Mom you're
not going to Die, yes I' am,
I've been hiding it from you
for the past three days it's
Cancer.
Gorgy, but listen to me.
Death is only a doorstep
away, use caution when
entering all doors, Sniff,
mom why did you hide that
from me George cried, I had
too, it was the only way to
make you focus on the task,
and now I'm telling you to
watch out!

OK, mom, what's that
beeping noise, I'm in the
hospital George, the doctors

say I'll be lucky if I make it
through the night, What!!!
This is happening too fast,
and I'm at work. I love you
mom, I'm going to come see
you after work, don't worry
sweetie, just worry about
yourself. I'm hooked to all
kind of machines I'm as
good as I can be, for the
time being, you got more
facing you my Gorgy, I have
to go now .....Click, Mom?
Mom?

Oh shit, this is the worst shit
you want to hear at work,
ugh let me hurry up back to
Doug, Sniff. As he walked
up the stairs that lead to the
dock, he heard faint crying,
he ran and then opened the
door

And was met with a rag

over his mouth then Blacked-out. Moments later he awakened to find his wrist and ankles was the nail to the floor. George thought what the hell as he laid flat on the floor. Then suddenly, he turned his head and saw Doug laid across from him nailed down as well with tape over his mouth mumbling something. George decided in his head to scream, hmm then he realizes his mouth was also taped as well, then by looking around he had an idea what was Paul planning for us as then he started tearing up crying and pleading, but his words didn't pass by the tape. *First thing, is this mic on? I want to say it's nice to be back here and to let you know I'm*

*the starter and the closer,
and wanted to give a special
thanks to George, for
drawing the attention of the
authorities to this building
and to Dan for having a nail
gun,* said Paul as he
clapped. *When I first started
to learn how to use the
rotary machine, I always
wondered what it would
look like to use a raw block
on human flesh. Sick as it
may be, I felt maybe I was a
little off, then after killing
the first couple of people, I
realized I was off, and by
being one that's off, it's
quite reasonable in our
world to have those
thoughts. Sorry for
rambling, I need to get to
business because we might
have unwanted guest due to
our workplace snitch. I'm*

going to peel back your tape for any last words. You might want me to tell your family friends or the local media, etc.... blah blah blah .let's start with you, Doug. Paul walked over to him and then leaned over *saying you know what? this would have been a good day to take off, but ah that "Big mouth bitch" makes it hard on the employee's to take off, oops oh well that's blood under the bridge or baler. Ok, you have five seconds no screaming, or I'll put the tape back and kick you in the nuts, even though that wouldn't be as painful compared to what I have planned for you.*

Ok, your five seconds starts now "rip" goes the tape.

Could you tell my fiancé I love her and my mom? *Ok, times up* then he resealed the tape. The *answer is no, how could I? Don't know them.* Paul stood up with a smile and walk over to George then squatted over him saying *you should have stayed at my house that morning. It would have been a less brutal death. Well you know that phrase, a hard head make's a soft behind, not in this case a hard head leave's a flatted skull,* then he laughed then stopped and said *five seconds,* Rip "Fuck you Paul" you selfish son of a bitch. *Oh, you must have met my mother, well my father is no prize either, you see how I turned out, Ha Ha and your Times up,* as he sealed the tape on George. *Since I like you, George, I'll let you go last.* Paul stood up *and his muscles cracked.*

Ah, I must be getting old as He walks over to put on his Tyvek suit, *do you think these outfits are made to protect people from dangerous stuff? Kind of funny, knowing that I am the hazard to people's health* said, Paul, as he walked to the rotary and wrapped his hands around the handles to tilt it back and rolled it over to Doug.
Oh well, it had to come to this. No Remorse, Nor Apologies...... He took off the stripping pad with just the metal Block with points. He moved the rotary right over Doug's head and said

Lets Rock and Roll like Chuck Berry.
Then started squeezing the handle, so the block was spinning like a car wheel going twenty miles an hour. As Doug laid there unable to move or scream he could only feel the wind of the block spinning over him before tickling his nose then tearing away the flesh off his face then grinding his skull down to a Bloody flat plate.

As Paul moved the machine to see what he had done with childlike glee. George ripped his sleeves away from the nails and ran frantically off the dock, *OH shit he didn't stick around, damn this looks abstract* as he laid the machine down looking at his creation *I could be the next Warhol, da Vinci or Picasso of murder art.*

George took the tape from his mouth as he ran to find help and ended up at the security desk and to see no one was on post, where the fuck is everyone? He asked, shit I was so close to dying again!!! Then he walked to the stairwell he looked up and said "Hello....... Hello" then stepped up to the second floor and looked around and all the lights were out on the floor. So he cut them on to find anyone, he saw a couple people at their desk. So George ran to them and to his surprise they were all dead, oh man this is not good said,

George, as he walked around then reached for his cell phone, Oh Fuck that bastard took my phone.

I better call the cops on one of the office phones, Ring………. Ring Hello 9-1-1 what's your emergency Hi. My Name is George, I'm at work, and there are dead people everywhere please hurry the killer is in the building!!!!! Ok, I will send out a unit, I got the location, so stay put and don't be a hero, Ok thanks said George, then he headed to the lobby, looking over his shoulder for Paul. Minutes later he heard sirens, then the officers came through the door, George explained in a panic all that he knew, the guy is

Paul, He's the killer, I saw
him do it, there are bodies
all around, sorry my words
are jumbled like a martini.
Take a deep breath Son and
have a seat, tell me your
name. It's George, and I
work here as a night Janitor.
Nice to meet you George
and I want to let you know,
that you're safe now and
we're going to find him,
would you like a soda from
the vending machine, no
thanks I'm Good. Ok
everybody, "Attention"
Let's comb the building!
Better this time around said
the captain. I want every
nook and cranny searched,
lets search from the ceiling
tiles down to the floors for
this guy, he is clever, and
needs to be stopped. Um,
may I add some info? He

could have gone to the other building as well George Stated, Ok Thanks let me call for back up for help with the search in the other building.
Come with us and be our leader to show us around.
"George is dying tonight" a mass text was sent to everybody in George's contacts, so family and friends got really concerned and tried calling and texting him back. Messages: Hello George, are you ok? call me back when you get this, was one of the many texts that were sent back to him.

George entered the stairwell Bang! Bang! Shots rang out when the officers drew their guns, and George took cover, seconds later a lady came around the corner with a gun. Drop your weapon, or we will shoot!!! She complied by dropping it and holding her hands up and looked at the officers and said I shot at him, I know at least 5 times. One of the bullets had to hit him!!! It happened so fast, like a mouse running through the kitchen. That Bastard tried to come right at me but shot him, and he ran off somewhere, he may not be dead, but he's hurting somewhere, is that gun registered asked the Officer, yes, it is, and what is your name? That fucker killed my brother said, Jane. Oh, I'm so sorry to hear that said George. Thanks, she said with a smile, I told him to be careful meeting people online. I had a feeling in my heart that it wouldn't end well Jane Explained while shaking her head, well sorry for your loss ma'am said the captain, just sit here in the lobby and collect yourself while we find him, ok thank you. (Static Noise) we learned that the culprit was hit look for any blood trails because it would lead you to him. (Static Noise) Rodger that sir.

I hate cases like these, if it weren't for anti-acids, I would have blown up years ago, Jane looked at the officer with the "what is this man talking about" look written all over her face. Are there any hidden doors in the building that you know of Sir?

Um, give me a sec, in the fifth-floor men's bathroom, said George, ok let us get ahead of you in case we need to fire shots, Ok? As they got off on the fifth floor they had their weapons drawn, Knock knock. If anyone's in here, come out with your hands up! After five seconds the officers charged in and George followed. In the last stall, the Officers found three butchered bodies. George turned to his left and saw blood smeared handprint from the side of this panel behind the bathroom door. "LOOK AND SEE WHAT'S IN THERE"! George yelled in a panic to the officers.

One officer stood on the left
side of the trap door to jar it
while the others clicked and
aimed at the door. The
officer at the door counted
off with his fingers to three
and pulled the door open.
Noises came from the small
door as everyone stood back
as something crawled out
the whole screaming like it
was in pain or being born
not knowing what to think
as it hit the floor and lunged
they started unloading
bullets at it, by feeling
threatened they had no
choice but to kill.

As the smoke poured from
the bullet-holes, they turned
over the body. George
looked at the body and said
that's not Paul! He still
alive, he said in a scared

tone, don't worry son, we will get him!! As the officers went to the other areas in the building the paramedics were just arriving as cops discover bodies from floor to floor.

Shit, I made it out alive, good thing the other building had a shower, and there were some Guy's clothes in the locker. I better hurry up because the cops will be over here in a second, I'm glad I smell better, I can't believe I lived in a hole for days on end, I walked straight out of the front lobby, and no one even noticed me.

Hope I fair as well outside, here we go, oh shit the cops are right there, let me walk the other way. I don't remember the street looking like this, oh well it's better than jail. Wow is it chilly outside I hope I don't catch pneumonia, knowing I just got out of the shower. I kept walking, I didn't run into anyone, strange indeed then suddenly, I saw a couple of ladies across the street walking the opposite direction but not paying them no mind as I kept on. Until I notice them Laughing, I look down at myself making sure my fly wasn't open, but if they could see that they must have a telescopic vision. Then I notice a group of guys walking across the street, going the same direction as the girls then the guys started laughing as well. Fuck them I said to myself and kept on my journey, not knowing where I was headed, I didn't care, and it felt good for the first time in weeks.

If I get picked up for murder, I'll say I didn't do it, or maybe I'll play the nutcase role so they won't give me the chair, oh I forgot Minnesota don't have the death penalty, so I'm good. Damn this walk is taking forever. I finally see somebody on my side of the street maybe they have a cigarette after the kind of day I had, sure could use a smoke, even though I haven't before, well I never killed till recently, so it's best to start now with all the bad habits all at once.

"Ha Ha Ha" *that laughter got louder, but not to worry getting a cigarette is our goal. More Laughter broke out, and it sounds close, but I won't turn around got to talk to the guy ahead of me, let me speed up Ha Ha Ha the Laughter sounds even closer fuck I can feel their breath on my neck and it smell, hey where did that guy go? Damn, I want to smoke, damn to busy looking at the cracks in the pavement.*

Hey, let's check all the Janitors closet suggested George, sure said the detective, do you have all the keys, yes, I do sir and by the way, it's just one key that opens them all replied George.   Let's go up to the sixth floor and work our way down, ok sir. As they headed down, they ran across a couple of bodies stashed in some of the Closets. Damn, I trained those girls less than a month ago Damn, Sorry George.

No Problem officer, it's just that (Static) Captain we found something, where are you? (Static) First Floor Electrical Room, Ok copy that (Static).
Let me turn around to see who's laughing at me Paul turned around to find most of his victims standing right before him Still laughing, *stop it, stop laughing at me. You guys are dead, I killed all of you, you're gone, and I'm alive Ha.* Suddenly, the Ground Creaked then

opened, and Nate Grabbed Paul's legs and Pulled Then the others tackled him down into the Hole into the earth AAhhhh Paul screamed and fought his way till he submitted then the ground closed behind them.

He's in here …Damn as George's eyes gazed upon the body in the room, which is that? One of the officers asked George exhaled with the biggest breath Yes, it's Him "Paul Nelson," it looked like he was cleaning his own mess from the bullet wounds, and that's why he was holding that rag, and what's that in his other hand. It's a picture, of a little Boy and a girl.

That was Paul as a kid and

my little sister who died in a
freak accident a while ago.
Said Paul's brother, and
took the photo from his
hand, turned to his fellow
officers and said, give me a
moment alone please, Ok
sir, as he closed the door he
looked, kneeled and said
Paul why? You could have
called me, then shook his
head and asked, if you
needed to talk or a place to
stay anything. I know we
weren't very good to you,
but we were just goofy kids
following orders. Wherever
you are, please forgive us,
in a way we are responsible
for how you ended up he
sighed, rest in peace my bro,
Love you and teared up.

He opened the door, I'm
done he said with a tremble

in his voice. Ok, this case is closed said the captain. I think we all should go to the lobby take it all in and thank you for all your help team. Hi, noted Jane to the handsome man walking with the cops, hello my name is George so......you shot him, and I wanted to give you a hug to thank you for stopping the murderous rampage, you're welcome, is he dead? Yeah, George Explained.   Jane Smiled and hugged George again, and they both sighed aloud. Would you like to go and get some coffee?

As in life, in the very foundation. The middle holds everything together, from a House, Sports teams, Automobiles, table legs, beds, Life, etc..... Imagine the world without the center. Pretty scary and incomplete. So, you would think that the middle child would hold the very core of a family together, Right? Or do they ever get a chance too?

THE END

DEDICATION

Though they left us too soon, they live on forever in our hearts and minds: Shirley, Rosalind, Roy, Robert and Ronald "Poncho"Kinchen, Nancy McKinney,Georgia, Charlie and Ron Elumn, Max (Doodle) Kinchen, Wes Craven, George A Romero Kevin L. Nordstrom, Marianne (Poly-styrene) Elliot-Said and Ariane (Ari-Up) Forster.